*A
Harlequin
Romance*

THE SPANISH GRANDEE

by

KATRINA BRITT

Harlequin Books

TORONTO • LONDON • NEW YORK • AMSTERDAM • SYDNEY • WINNIPEG

Original hardcover edition published in 1975
by Mills & Boon Limited

SBN 373-01969-6

Harlequin edition published May, 1976

CHAPTER ONE

VENETIA had gone to sleep with the idea flickering through her mind. She awoke to find it had fixed itself there firmly. Why should she not take the job her sister Carolyn had changed her mind about accepting? Two years in Spain typing out the memoirs of a Spanish nobleman. All that hot sun and Spanish courtesy flicked away by one wave of Carolyn's perfectly manicured hand. All because of the Spanish grandee.

Venetia linked her hands behind her tawny head and gazed up reminiscently from her pillow at the ceiling of her room. Six years ago the Spanish grandee had entered her life on a short cataclysmic visit never to be repeated.

Venetia did not remember her parents, who had been killed in a car crash when she was two years old. Carolyn, her sister, had been four. They had been brought up by their father's only sister, Aunt Dorothy, in her lovely Sussex home with its spacious orchards and paddocks.

The house next door, Tamor Hall, had belonged to Squire Tamor whose two sons, Julian and Simon, had been very kind to the two little orphaned girls. They had taught them to swim in their outdoor swimming pool, taken them fishing and riding and had beaten them unmercifully at tennis.

The Tamors had a Latin look. Julian was swarthy with black hair and eyes, very handsome. He was tall and lean, whereas Simon was slightly stocky with a round cherubic face. Simon had been nineteen, Julian twenty, when they had returned home from college for the summer vacation bringing with them a distant cousin, and Venetia and Carolyn, fourteen and sixteen respectively at the time, had been invited to spend the day with them at Tamor Hall. Wearing swimsuits beneath their towelling robes, they had strolled through the gap in the hedge between the two houses which both families had used for years and had reached the steps leading down to the swimming pool at Tamor Hall. There they had halted to gaze up open-mouthed at the young Greek god poised high above them on the springboard.

Carolyn, red-haired, green-eyed and long-legged, had murmured esctatically:

"Wow! Where did he come from?"

Venetia, her tawny eyes fixed upon rippling muscles beneath a skin of bronze satin, had held her breath and watched him do a triple somersault into the pool.

"A Spanish grandee, without a doubt," she had commented, taking in the small Van Dyke beard, precision-cut, which gave him a sardonic expression as he had surfaced from the water. Loose-limbed, with a fluid grace, he had vaulted effortlessly on to the side of the pool to push back the black, crisply curling hair and smile at them with shattering charm.

To Venetia the tall, lithe figure, the intense black eyes set beneath straight dark brows in an eagle-like countenance, had held all the ingredients from which romantic dreams were made. Age twenty-four, he was studying Economics at London University, and his name was Ramón de Biver y Aldenez.

At fourteen, Venetia had been too young and naïve to form a very deep impression. She remembered him as being charmingly courteous with the exciting male vitality of a man at the top of his form. That he had enjoyed life had been obvious, for he had that congenital gift of putting his personality across to others with a magnetic force.

Carolyn, on the other hand, had made a dead set at him. "I'm mad about that beard, and his eyes send prickles down my spine," she had confided to Venetia. "Julia says his family own vast estates in Spain and are disgustingly rich."

The Spanish grandee, however, had treated Carolyn's marked preference for his company with an amused tolerance and when he had strolled nonchalantly out of their lives at the end of the summer vacation without asking them to write to him, her ego had been badly dented.

"Who does he think he is, the arrogant creature," she had fumed, and Venetia had smiled wisely, knowing by experience that Carolyn's sudden crushes on the opposite sex were usually of short duration.

6

Six years had passed, during which Aunt Dorothy had died and her estate, left to her in trust for a nephew by her late husband, had passed on. Venetia and Carolyn shared a flat in London where Carolyn, ever ambitious, had worked her way up to private secretary to a young executive of a large concern.

Venetia had worked with the old family solicitor until his death a week previously. She was now out of a job.

A year ago Squire Tamor had been killed in a hunting accident and Julian was struggling to run the estate at a profit despite crippling death duties. His romance with Carolyn had been on and off throughout the years with nothing really settled between them. Julian, Venetia knew, would marry Carolyn like a shot had she not been loth to marry a poor man. It was while Lucian was away visiting his brother Simon, now farming in Canada, that Carolyn had seen the advertisement in *The Times*. A certain Señor Jorge Fadrillo Moreno required the services of a typist for a period of two years. Applicants had to apply by letter along with suitable references. The address was Santa Marta, with Barcelona as the nearest city.

Carolyn, remembering that the Spanish grandee came from somewhere in the vicinity, suddenly decided to apply for the job. Everything would be plain sailing if she was accepted, because they had already booked an early spring holiday in Spain. The plan was for Venetia to travel with her sister for a fortnight's holiday before returning to look for another job. In due course Carolyn had been accepted and all arrangements had been made for them to leave at the end of the week, which brought Venetia's thoughts up to the previous evening in the flat.

She had washed her hair and was rubbing it briskly with a towel when Carolyn had burst in.

"What do you think?" she cried excitedly. "I met Lady Rollsmere at the lunch given for the board members and she told me that the Spanish grandee has bought a luxury apartment overlooking Hyde Park!" She sank down on the divan and lighted a cigarette, exhaling and savouring the good news with her lovely head thrown back, her green eyes glittering oddly. "And there's more to come. Guess what?"

Venetia paused, towel in hand, and shook her still damp head.

"His father is dead and Ramón is now a Conde and fabulously rich. I can't wait to see him again!"

Venetia said calmly, "But you won't see him, because you'll be in Spain. Are you forgetting that we leave this weekend?"

Carolyn blew out a line of smoke and stated determinedly, "You don't imagine I shall go now? It's all off."

For several shattering moments Venetia had been bereft of speech. She remembered staring stupidly at the unrepentant lovely face.

"But you can't do that!" she had cried in protest. "It's all arranged, my holiday with you and . . . and everything." She had bit her lip, thinking of all the time she had put in pressing all their clothes and packing them. "Besides," she added desperately, "Señor Moreno will be expecting you."

Carolyn had slipped off her shoes and wriggled her toes, in no way abashed.

"There's no reason why you shouldn't go on your holiday as planned and make an excuse. Tell Señor Moreno I'm ill or something. He can always engage someone else." The green eyes following the thin trail of cigarette smoke to the ceiling hardened. "He kept me waiting long enough for his reply to my application."

Reasonably, Venetia said, "He could have been checking up on your references. Don't forget that you told him to refer to the Spanish grandee for one of your references. As Don Ramón was probably in London at the time negotiating for his flat he might not have been available to corroborate your story."

But Carolyn had not been listening. Her lovely face had softened as she dreamed of Ramón, who was now a Conde. Venetia continued to rub her hair and had wished that Lucien was there. At least he could have met his rival on home ground. Venetia was very fond of Julian and Simon and would have done anything to save them pain.

"How do you know that the Spanish grandee isn't already

8

married?" she said grimly. "Some of those Spanish noblemen are betrothed at an early age to someone of their parents' choice. I shouldn't build up my hopes if I were you."

Carolyn's eyes had gleamed like emeralds. "Ramón isn't married – I asked Lady Rollsmere. She's planning to give a party for him!" The very thought of it made Carolyn's mouth curve with pleasurable anticipation. "I might even take him down a peg or two for treating me so casually when he was at Tamor Hall."

Venetia had stared at her aghast. "Do you mean to say you've carried a grudge against the man all these years? At least he was honest. He didn't lead you on with false promises which he had no intention of keeping. That's what makes me think he could have a *novia*."

"A fiancée?" Carolyn scoffed openly. "Don't be silly. Why, he would have been married by now if that was so. He was twenty-four six years ago, which makes him thirty now – a man of experience, terribly exciting, with castles in Spain. What more can a girl ask?"

She stubbed out the butt of her cigarette and stretched up her arms luxuriously as Venetia began to brush her hair.

"I wish you luck. I would have been content to spend two years in Spain. Just fancy missing two winters here!" Venetia paused, hairbrush held in mid-air thoughtfully. "What about your job? You've given your notice."

"Oh, haven't I told you?" Carolyn smiled faintly. "I meant to. I have another job as secretary to a beauty consultant who lives in the same block of luxury flats as the Spanish grandee." She leaned back on her hands and her smile widened. "Don't you think that was clever of me?"

Venetia had quivered, a trifle bewildered at the sudden change of plan.

"I don't know," she had answered, lowering the hairbrush with a hand suddenly gone weak. "I only hope you know what you're doing and are not taking a step you might later regret."

Venetia, staring up at the ceiling of her room, knew from past experience that Carolyn never regretted anything. She had always been clever enough to turn every situation to her own advantage. Why should not she, Venetia, do the same? It was on this interesting thought that she left her bed.

Coffee had been made, the electric toaster filled and switched on, when Carolyn entered the kitchen for breakfast looking ultra-smart in a tan suit, beautifully cut, with a tiny green kerchief tied provocatively at the side of her elegant throat.

"Hurry with that toast. I'm late," she cried, taking her seat at the gay yellow formica-topped kitchen table.

But the urgency of her tones were for once unheeded by Venetia, who was lost in the magic of Spain, conjuring up visions of majestic landscapes, sprigged flower sun-dresses, huge earthenware pots of exotic blooms and hot golden sun.

"I've been thinking," she said, pouring out two cups of freshly made coffee and passing one to her sister. "This job you've turned down in Spain. Would you mind if I went in your place?"

Carolyn, who was rummaging in her handbag for cigarettes, looked up sharply. "Out of the question. I've put a good word in for you to my boss and he's going to give you a trial. It will mean a substantial rise on what you've been earning."

Venetia reached for the slices of toast popping up from the toaster, spread them liberally with butter and placed them on a plate in the centre of the table.

Then she said quietly, "I wish you'd told me what you had in mind. I could have saved you the trouble of speaking for me. I might as well tell you now that I would never entertain the idea of working for your boss. I can't stand him. Like most young executives, he's pompous and too full of his own importance. I'm sorry, but I don't want the job."

Carolyn's green eyes widened in disbelief and she put down her coffee cup with a thud. "Of all the ungrateful creatures! You must be stark, staring mad to turn your nose up at a job that lots of girls would give a year's salary for. It might never come your way again." Her nostrils dilated with anger. "I've worked hard to make myself into the perfect secretary and I could give you all the gen so that you would have it all at your, finger tips. You wouldn't need to put a foot wrong. It's a ready-made job with an excellent salary. You'd better think it over."

"I don't need to think it over." Belligerently defensive, Venetia kept her voice low and firm. "It might be the perfect job, but it isn't for me," adding to make it more clear, "Besides, I should be jumping the queue, and don't tell me there aren't girls in your office expecting to be offered the first chance of the job."

Carolyn reached for a finger of toast. "You forget they won't have the briefing I intend to give you. Be a sport and take it." She put on her most winsome smile. "You see, I've told him you'll be very happy to take the job. It made it easier to give in my notice by offering him a good replacement."

Venetia hardened. She put down her coffee, having lost the taste for it, and looked her straight in the eye. "That's your fault. You're too ready to use other people for your own ends. I'm declining the offer. Now do you mind answering my question?"

Carolyn was deliberately obtuse. "What question?"

"I asked if you minded my taking your place in this job with Señor Moreno. The Spanish grandee taught me quite a lot of Spanish when he was at Tamor Hall."

"So he did." Carolyn's green eyes narrowed thoughtfully. "Do you know, I'd forgotten all about it. Yes, it might be a good idea for you to take the job. I couldn't have you staying here with Ramón around. You might try to persuade him to give you more lessons, and that would only queer my pitch, wouldn't it? You may go with my blessing. Now I must be off. I don't know what I'm going to say to George about you refusing the job."

Hastily Carolyn repaired her make-up, thrust things into her handbag and made for the door.

Venetia said, smiling, "Tell him I have a job lined up in Spain. I'm sure he'll understand. You said yourself that the man is a sun-worshipper. I'll send you my share of the rent of the flat each quarter – and thank you."

Carolyn's vicious slam of the door only served to bring a

gurgle of laughter to Venetia's lips. Leaving her chair, she waltzed around the kitchen with joy.

Venetia boarded the plane on a chill February morning and took her seat by the window with a curious feeling of finality. Far below was the moving patchwork of green and brown fields interlaced with arterial roads along which cars looked like coloured beetles crawling along in an endless file. The plane turned swooping like a huge bird before it began to gain height.

After the first tenseness of the take-off, Venetia was beginning to relax more and more as her shoulders softened and some of the rigid feeling in the muscles of her neck slackened. Eyes closed, she leaned back in her seat, hoping she was doing the right thing. If it turned out wrongly she had only herself to blame. It was all her own doing, that frantic rush for extras needed for the longer stay, two years instead of the two weeks she had prepared for.

Gradually the murmur of voices around her sank into her consciousness. One deep voice to her right across the aisle – a deep brown voice, beautifully cultured – drew her eyes sideways to look across the empty seat beside her.

The plane, she noticed, was almost full, with only a few vacant seats including the one beside her. The air hostess moved away from the dark brown voice with his order for refreshment, giving Venetia a clear view of the owner.

Her first impression was one of length and leanness, a handsome clear-cut profile, deeply tanned, and black crisp hair covering an arrogantly poised head. Obviously a foreigner despite his perfect English, she decided, noting all the signs of good breeding and strength of character in the high cheek-bones of his dark face. Strange yet familiar in a way she could not yet define. Her eyes lingered on the strong brown hand beneath snow white cuffs before they widened at the sight of the signet on the little finger of that left hand.

Venetia's heart was now beating suffocatingly in her throat. She gave a start and found that he was returning her scrutiny with a proud, outrageously cool regard from black expressive eyes. With the warm blood rushing to her face in waves, Venetia tilted her chin towards her window to fix her eyes on the blue sky beyond. She had met him before. But where? He was certainly not a business tycoon, for he wore a pale grey suit, faultlessly cut, with a careless elegance, the hallmark of a born aristocrat. He was a fine-looking man around thirty, she would say, with the blackest eyes she had ever seen beneath straight dark brows. His nose was distinctive with a barely perceptible arch above a mobile mouth which, Venetia was sure, could curve mockingly. His chin, clean-shaved, was firm and determined; a dangerous man to cross but an exciting one all the same.

All this Venetia had taken in on her second perusal of his face. When she whipped up enough courage to steal a third glance surreptitiously under her lashes across the aisle, he had taken a monogrammed cigarette case from an inside pocket and was lighting a cigarette. Against the light from his window his profile presented a nobility of line which could have graced a gold coin. Now with a beard, she pondered, and her breath rasped . . . A beard! That was it – he had shaved off his beard. The Spanish grandee. He was the Spanish grandee minus his beard.

Venetia was back at Tamor Hall, seeing again the magnificent bronze figure somersaulting through the air, the practised ripple of muscles cleaving through the water, the slow charming smile as he had emerged showing excellent white teeth. That precision-cut beard of his university days was no more.

Good heavens! Here he was on his way to Spain and Carolyn was expecting him to be in London. Venetia was so upset that she must have gone a trifle lightheaded, for, leaning across the empty seat, she acted completely out of character and addressed him.

"Excuse me, I don't suppose you'll remember me. We met years ago – six, to be exact."

The black eyes turned slowly to hold her gaze with a cool arrogance with the silence between them becoming all the more acute because of the chatter and laughter around them.

Borrowing a little of his coolness, Venetia went on, "I can

13

see you don't remember me." Her mouth twitched impishly. Really, she thought, the man thinks I'm making a pass at him! The arrogant creature! The urge to jolt him from his pedestal was too much. Her voice was as smooth as cream, her tawny eyes danced. "And I wasn't even hiding under a beard."

"Was I?" indifferently.

"Yes indeed."

Another silence during which his face remained inscrutable. Then he clicked his long tapering brown fingers comprehendingly. "Ah, I have it! Tamor Hall. Now let me think." Were the black eyes openly teasing for a second? "You and your sister next door."

Venetia nodded. "That's right. You are Señor Ramón de Biver y Aldanez." The dimple in her cheek became more marked. "Minus the beard."

He inclined his dark head slightly. He did not unbend, but his manner was less frigid, more friendly. "And you are . . ." For an instant his eyes rested upon the tawny hair. "Miss Venetia Mellor minus the ponytail."

She coloured, recalling the freckles and long-legged gawkiness of six years ago. "Correct," she admitted before putting a hand to her mouth in dismay. "Goodness, I forgot! You're not Señor any more – you're a Conde. I beg your pardon."

To her surprise a shutter descended upon his face and in an effort to lift it she hastened on. "I mean, about your father. I shouldn't have mentioned the fact that you're now a Conde, only you see . . . I. . . ." She swallowed, finding it impossible to keep the sympathy from softening her eyes, and tried again. "What I wanted to say was how very sorry I was to hear about your father. I remember how you used to write to him every day. You were so close, and you must miss him dreadfully."

Something flashed in the dark eyes and was instantly veiled. "My father died two years ago. You are right, I do miss him," he answered evenly.

"I'm so sorry," she said sincerely. "You know that Squire Tamor died?"

Again he inclined his head. Venetia was finding it hard to

meet the intent gaze of those dark eyes and she lowered her lashes wondering why that mobile mouth which, she remembered, used to smile with a mixture of charm and humour, should remain so grim.

It was he who broke the silence. "You are travelling alone, Miss Mellor?" he enquired, looking pointedly at the empty seat beside her.

Her nerves tightened. Miss Mellor. Six years ago it had been Venetia and Ramón. But he was now a Conde. Even so, she would not have thought him to be a snob. Somehow it hurt very much.

Retreating imperceptibly, she said, "My sister Carolyn couldn't come with me as planned. Something . . . er . . . came up at the last moment and she cancelled her holiday."

She suppressed an hysterical giggle, wondering what on earth he would say if she told him why Carolyn was staying behind.

"Cigarette?" He flicked open his cigarette case and she shook her head.

"No, thanks, I don't smoke," she answered. Then in case he should regard her as being unsophisticated, she added hastily, "I don't really enjoy it."

He looked at her with an expression which she could not analyse – searching – quizzical – mocking? She did not know. There was a rather bitter pull about his mouth and she wondered why. Then she remembered that Carolyn had mentioned him to Señor Moreno as a reference. Did he know about it? It was possible that he had not been at home at the time and that the Señor had not yet contacted him in the matter.

This put her in a quandary, wondering how much he knew about Carolyn applying for the job. It was impossible to ask him point blank and also impossible to be frank with him without betraying Carolyn.

He had put his cigarette case away and looked at her again. He did not say a word, just looked at her until her heart began to lurch in the strangest way. It sort of turned over, then missed a beat. No man had ever made a direct contact with her heart before. It was uncanny.

He said at last, "You are going to Spain, Miss Mellor, like most of the English do these days?"

Venetia felt relegated to the tourist class and her resentment set a distinct edge to her voice. "No. I'm hoping to work in Spain for the next two years."

The dark eyebrows lifted. "Hoping?"

"Yes. I haven't had any experience in the kind of work I'm expecting to do, but I think I'm quite capable of doing it."

He said politely, "May one ask the nature of your work?"

"I've been engaged as a typist by a Señor Moreno of Santa Marta," she replied.

He looked startled for a moment, then gave his attention to the air hostess who came along with his drink. The small table in front of him was pulled out and he settled down with his newspaper, apparently forgetting her existence.

Venetia let her head fall back in her chair. What rotten luck to bump into the Spanish grandee of all people, especially when she had imagined him to be in London. What Carolyn would say she could not imagine. Unless he was taking a quick flip back home until the details of the purchase of his London flat were complete. Was it a bad omen? It was certainly a bad start to her new job. During the short time he had been at Tamor Hall they had never been close. He had taught her Spanish at odd intervals, laughed at her awful pronunciation until she had had to improve it. But that was all. Somehow he had always kept himself aloof from the rest of the crowd even while joining in.

His attitude had not changed. He was a man who lived up to a certain code, a code he would not change come hell or high water. He would not take to deception lightly, and was not that precisely what she was doing? Too late now to wish she had contacted Señor Moreno to ask if he would accept her in her sister's place. Venetia closed her eyes. The beat of her heart had quietened as the sound of the plane's engines pulsed louder and louder in her ears. Her whole body seemed to be pulsing with noise and gradually she slept.

The jolt of the plane landing again on solid earth roused her She had arrived. The swift short run, and the passengers were unfastening their seat belts. Unfastening her own, Venetia was aware of the Spanish grandee looking across the aisle.

"Wait for me when you have gone through the Customs," he said unsmilingly. "I will give you a lift to your destination."

Venetia bristled. "Thanks, but it won't be necessary. I'm sure Señor Moreno will have sent some kind of conveyance. If not, I can always take a taxi. I wouldn't entertain the idea of taking you out of your way."

He said coolly, "You are not taking me out of my way. I have been requested to give you a lift into Santa Marta. Señor Moreno, your prospective employer, is my uncle by marriage."

Venetia had the sensation of wallowing in quicksands. Suddenly she was very angry with him for being so secretive not realizing that she had behaved precisely the same towards him. So he knew everything! In that moment she heartily disliked him. The flash of anger in her tawny eyes did not escape him. He rose to his feet and gestured for her to precede him down the aisle.

For a moment she hesitated, rising from her seat below his six foot odd height to hoist her shoulder bag more firmly in place. The faint bow, the mere movement of his dark arrogant head was so supercilious that she swept out before him to march down the aisle, head high.

Outside the airport the long black car with the coat of arms on the door stood ostentatiously empty. He put her case in the boot, seated her in the front seat and slid in behind the wheel in silence. Blinking a little at the strong light through her window, Venetia gazed out on strange country. The bright sun after the candlelight variety of February sun she had left behind was startlingly glaring. In the heat haze the pale pink and whitewashed building huddled behind closed shutters, palm trees rustled, a cathedral loomed in isolated splendour, an incongruous background for policemen armed for any emergency, then the dark foliage among which oranges and lemons gave a gay touch. Venetia gazed with awe, enchanted as a child on a much promised outing as her eyes became accustomed to the new quality of light, widening as they took in first impressions.

The Spanish grandee handled the big car, as she would imagine he would handle most things, with smoothness and skill. He did not speak until they had left the wide boulevards behind with the towns and suburbs and were speeding towards the sharks' teeth of mountains biting the blue sky. Venetia gazed out dreamily on an expanse of open brown land, sun-baked terracotta houses of Moorish design and grilled windows. The air was filled with wood smoke and rosemary and the only sound above the car engine was the tinkle of goat bells or the mooing of a cow.

Enchanted as she had been by the scenery, Venetia had also been acutely aware of the man at her side. The faint emanation of his masculine fragrance exercised a predominate force which moved her profoundly. Minus the Van Dyke beard, his good looks were more arresting than ever. The last six years had, if anything, given an added distinction to the high-cheek-boned planes of his face, so striking with its straight dark brows, black eyes and thick crisp hair.

His unexpected appearance on the plane had unnerved her, and the strangeness of her surroundings added to it. It was not until he spoke that she realized that instead of sitting back in the luxurious leather upholstery, she was perched on the edge of her seat clutching it with both hands.

"Are you nervous of travel, Miss Mellor?" he asked sardonically.

Venetia kept her eyes fixed on the rapidly unwinding dusty road ahead, refusing to look at him. "Not really," she replied, wishing she knew what lay ahead at the end of the journey. "You're speeding though."

He said ironically, "Fifty kilometres is hardly going at a suicidal rate. Let me console you with the fact that I have a clean licence and have kept free of accidents until now."

Venetia sank back in her seat and stole a glance at his set profile. He looked immensely strong and every inch a Conde giving a lift to a would-be employee of his uncle. That was how he would regard her from now on, never again as a social equal swimming in the pool at Tamor Hall. But who cared? She certainly did not. She might never set eyes on him again once he had deposited her at his uncle's door.

She said hopefully, "Is it much further to Santa Marta?"

"Another hour. I take it my uncle is expecting you and not your sister Carolyn?"

Their eyes met briefly and she felt the frightened leap of her pulse. The words came with the force of a blow beneath the belt. She surfaced and gasped for air.

"No. There . . . there was no time to explain. You see, Carolyn had the offer of a better job, so she decided to take it at the last moment and . . . and I came in her place."

"I see. I am surprised she is not married or at least has a *novio*."

Oh dear, she thought. Was this a leading question? How much did he know of Carolyn's affairs? Did he know of her association with Julian? Though why should he? He had not kept in touch with the Tamors, since he did not attend Squire Tamor's funeral. He was only a distant cousin and obviously kept his distance.

She answered warily, "Carolyn isn't married, nor is she engaged."

He said suavely, "I am surprised you did not make a match of it with my cousins, Julian and Simon."

"We're close friends. I suppose you know Julian is trying to make the estate pay. He's gone to visit Simon in Canada to study farming methods there. Simon is doing well on a farm of his own."

They had been climbing steadily, for now the plains lay well behind them, swallowed in a soft haze of heat. Before them, in the distance, was a village, and Venetia glimpsed the spire of a cathedral church and houses fashioned years ago by craftsmen of a bygone age. Cooler air penetrating the car settled on her warm skin and she shivered inwardly. The sense of chill came more from the knowledge that she was skating on thin ice. While she had spoken the truth about Carolyn being unattached, she knew that Julian regarded her as his property and would not hesitate to say so. There had been no exchange of rings and Venetia had always felt that Carolyn had no scruples where Julian was concerned. Had a wealthy man happened along when Carolyn had been in one of her moods, she would not have hesitated at accepting him.

"You must have wanted the position very badly, to deceive my uncle. How long have you known about your sister's change of plan?" he asked evenly.

Venetia took him up sharply. "Deceive is rather a strong word." She hurried on, "Everything happened at once. There was very little time. In any case, I preferred to explain to Señor Moreno personally. I have the same qualifications as my sister, so I didn't see the need to complicate matters over the telephone or by a letter which wouldn't have reached him in time anyway."

"Indeed. Are you running away from something or someone?" There was a brief pause, then he said slowly, "Have you a *novio*, Miss Mellor?"

"No, I have not, neither am I running away from anything or anybody. I intend to tell Señor Moreno the truth when the opportunity arises," she vouchsafed with dignity. "In any case, as employer and employee we shall hardly be on christian name terms. Maybe it was silly of me, but there it is. I do not usually go around deceiving people."

"I am sorry," he said, but did not sound in the least so. "It was an unfortunate word to use. You acted impulsively. But you are young and the young are ever impulsive."

She glanced at his unyielding profile. "If you have ever wanted anything badly, you'll understand."

He let this pass and said sardonically, "Sailing under false colours can be very embarrassing socially, especially if you form any close friendships with the opposite sex. They will want to know your first name."

Venetia swallowed on a dry throat and hoped he was not going to be awkward. "I came out to Spain to work, not to look for a husband. You could do me a favour."

20

He favoured her with a swift glance. "Yes?"

He had slid back behind his wall of reserve. Was it a presage of something more unpleasant in the offing? There had been moments, a day or so ago, when she had thought about him fleetingly, and had imagined how pleasant it would be to meet him again. At Tamor Hall he had talked to her, been kind and had taught her Spanish, punctuated by laughter. He had treated her like a small sister and she had loved his teasing. But he had been charming to everyone, especially Carolyn, who had demanded his attentions and had sulked when he had not been available. If only he would smile!

Venetia bit her lip and began, "Will you allow me to tell Señor Moreno who I am when we arrive? I realize it's putting you into a false position since your uncle knows, no doubt, that you are acquainted with Carolyn and myself. Would you introduce me as simply Miss Mellor?"

He said coldly, "Since I know your background I will accede to your request. Normally, it would have been none of my business whom my uncle chooses to employ. However, since he approached me in way of a reference, I am now involved. You must promise me to tell him at the first opportunity."

"Thanks. I'm more than grateful. Is . . . is Señor Moreno an understanding man?" she asked tentatively.

She glanced at his dark face and saw the semblance of a smile hovering about his well cut mouth. "Very." His voice sounded suddenly deep and warm. "You will find him very easy to work with."

In her relief she warmed towards him and her tongue loosened. "I'm so glad. You have no idea how grateful I am to you. I don't suppose you have any idea what it's like to want or need anything in life which wouldn't be yours for the asking."

He turned his head and looked at her very directly, and it struck her anew how incredibly dark his eyes were now very attractive. She blinked and looked away overwhelmed with a sudden shyness.

"So," he said, giving his attention to the road once more. "You think I can have everything I want or need out of life, that there is nothing that I am in need of at this present moment? This is most interesting. Tell me, Miss Mellor, what gives you that idea? Do I look smug and well blessed with everything which makes life worth living?"

Venetia blessed her unwary tongue for landing her in a tight corner, and endeavoured to wriggle out of it. "Well, shall we put it this way? Anyone like yourself, born with a silver spoon in your mouth, is usually blessed with enough of the world's goods to make life comfortable."

He said dryly, "Wealth can be a mixed blessing. Indeed, it can become a liability. You are very young, Miss Mellor, and like the young, regard money as the utmost importance."

"Not as important as health, happiness and . . . love, of course," she hastened on. "I was talking with your country in mind. A wealthy Spaniard usually has his life planned out for him down to the last detail, which could include a bride of his parents' choice. Is that not so?"

"Consequently he is very happy?" mockingly.

"He can come very near to it, since he's brought up to accept that way of life. I'm only speaking of you. It wouldn't do for me."

His eyebrows lifted sardonically. "No? Why not?"

"Because I could never marry a man I wasn't in love with."

"Love can begin with respect and flower after marriage," he said.

Venetia quivered. "And if it doesn't?"

"That is something we have to face with a light heart."

The half smile he gave her was wholly charming. Against it Venetia was powerless. He had turned the tables on her with that irresistible charm which, she was sure, knocked the *señoritas* over like ninepins to fall at his well shod feet. When he spoke again it was on a more superficial level, commenting on the scenery and pointing out objects of interest – a terra-cotta eighteenth-century church and monastery – a curiously shaped windmill – a huge grotesque cactus.

As the car ate up the miles, Venetia's heart grew colder and she dreaded the end of the journey when she would be assessed by the ultimate authority on her suitability for the job. Conversation was desultory as her anxiety became more acute. In the few brief glances Ramón had given her, she had noticed that his eyes remained unsmiling above the lightness of his voice. So it was hardly surprising that her own small, wavering smile was not spontaneously bright.

"You said giving me this lift wouldn't take you out of your way," she said, knowing her voice was edged with anger. But she did not care. "Do you reside in the vicinity?" She was prepared for the lift of the black, silky eyebrows and seethed with annoyance. How dared he treat her like . . . someone he had given a lift and nothing more?

"My estate is near the coast," he replied laconically.

He did not enlarge upon this and Venetia hoped it was far, far away from the Villa Alicia, his uncle's residence. She could not wait to get away from him. Maybe when they chanced to meet again she would feel less guilty, having had time to confess her little act of deception to Señor Moreno. Why worry, in any case? He could only refuse to engage her and send her home. She would find another post soon enough. There were plenty of jobs for typists, plenty of opportunities. It was only a matter of finding the right one.

Venetia kept her eyes resolutely ahead, seeing nothing but the road unwinding to some unknown destination. A ruined castle sped by where children played among the orange trees below the battlements. Then the village was looming ahead, filling the windscreen. Soon they were on a switchback of narrow winding streets before turning off on to a side road where no traffic save a few mules was to be seen. Gradually the grandeur of the landscape, the sense of serenity reaching out to the distant mauve peaks of the mountains lulled her into a state of acceptance of her fate. She was utterly calm when the car turned smoothly along a drive to draw up at the main entrance of the Villa Alicia. The slumbering silence was profound.

No Señor Moreno to welcome us, concluded Venetia, as she stepped from the luxurious car and welcomed the small respite in which to take in her surroundings.

CHAPTER TWO

THE Villa Alicia was a white-porticoed building crowned by a graceful tower. Deep awnings and closed shutters protected windows and loggias from the heat. They had driven under an archway into a courtyard with an enchanting well in the centre. A long balustraded gallery ran around three sides of it, protected by a steeply sloping roof, and plants, shrubs and flowers overflowed everywhere in earthenware pots.

Venetia took a deep breath as her eyes became accustomed to the sparkling clarity of light, the contrasting depth of shadows cast by a trellis of vine around white pillars supporting the porticoed entrance. The brass-studded, heavy door was open, the interior cool and dark after the glare of the sun.

As they went forward a woman came out of the house to greet them in the porch. Small, with black hair worn in Spanish fashion in wings over each temple to culminate into a knot at the nape of her neck, she wore a friendly air as demure as the black dress enhancing her small figure.

"*Buenos dias*, Ramón," she said in a pleasant, low voice, and he answered in crisp Spanish. She nodded and spoke urgently in the same soft low tones, and then Ramón turned to Venetia.

"Señor Moreno is indisposed, but Tia Matilde has prepared your room." The white smile flashed charmingly. "Tia Matilde, may I present the youngest of the charming Mellor sisters who helped to make my visit years ago to Tamor Hall so enjoyable and unforgettable? Miss Mellor, Doña Matilde, Don Jorge's sister."

Doña Matilde greeted her with such a shy apprehension that Venetia immediately warmed to her. "*Mucho gusto*, Doña Matilde," she said very carefully, trying out her Spanish, and was inclined to laugh because she had said it correctly.

Doña Matilde held her hand for a moment while she enquired if she had had a good journey, and Ramón strode off in search of the staff. She heard him address someone as Carlo.

"*Sirvace hacer subir equipaje la* Señorita Mellor," he ordered in crisp Spanish, and an elderly man appeared to go out to his car.

"Come," said Doña Matilde. "You must be tired after your journey. I will take you to your room."

While Ramón strode away presumably to see his uncle, Venetia allowed herself to be escorted up the wide shallow staircase set in the centre of a black and white tiled hall. The windows in the hall and at the head of the stairs were stained glass which gave a gentle dim quality of light so welcome after the glare outdoors. The atmosphere was cool and thoroughly restful to Venetia, who was too weary with travel to notice only a few details like the bowls of flowers artistically arranged on low tables beneath each window and the thick-carpeted corridor leading to her room.

Doña Matilde was saying, "We shall not expect you downstairs to dinner this evening as you will be much too tired. Pura will run your bath and bring you hot chocolate with a light meal. I hope you sleep well."

Alone in her room after Carlo had brought up her luggage and Pura, the little maid, had run her bath, Venetia pulled her wrap around her slim figure and with a strange feeling of unreality opened the shutters of her window to gaze out from her balcony to a gradually deepening twilight.

The immense sky, a serene, darkening, cloudless blue, the purple distances fading into the rugged contour of mountain ranges, was breathtaking. It seemed to Venetia that nothing moved, that she was gazing at a picture painted by a master hand. She drew in a contented breath of clean air. Here there was room to breathe, to think, to dream. Her tawny eyes tried to pierce the distant shadows. In what direction did the sea lie, the coast where the Spanish grandee had his estate? Really, she was an idiot to bother about him after the way he had treated her.

There was no likelihood of her ever seeing his home. He had been an unwilling escort to the villa of his uncle and had lost no

25

time in relinquishing his responsibility upon reaching the end of the journey. How strange that he had remained so cold, so aloof after their friendship of six years ago. His smile had only appeared at rare intervals and never for her during the whole journey, and that rather bitter pull to his mouth had brought a funny little nagging ache to her heart.

It was only too clear to one of her sensitive perception that he was not a happy man. Had the loss of his father wrought the change in him, or had some other tragedy occurred during the last six years to affect him so? Venetia gripped the rail of the balcony. The sun already had an orange tinge, bringing a darker heat and a heaviness which matched her mood. Already she was aware that her life had changed irrevocably. She was aware of danger lurking in the dimness; why else would her pulses quicken at the thought of him? How could she feel like this? This aching, this yearning, feeling his pain as acutely as though it was her own. The sensible thing to do was to admit that it had happened and to squash every possible spark before it kindled into an unquenchable flame.

Unhappily, she thought of the flat he had bought in London. Was it Carolyn after all? He had told Doña Matilde that the Mellor sisters had made his visit to Tamor Hall unforgettable. They would certainly make a handsome couple. Slowly she turned back into dusky room filled with coppery light and went to take her bath.

The insistent knocking penetrated her unconsciousness. Venetia opened her eyes and automatically bade whoever it was enter.

It was Pura, the little Andalusian maid, with her breakfast tray. She was well made and darkly swarthy with black eyes alive with curiosity.

"Did you sleep well, Miss Mellor?" she enquired as Venetia pushed herself up sleepily on her pillows, blinking a little at the strong beams of light thrusting between the slats of the window shutters.

"Wonderfully well, thank you, Pura," she replied with a smile as the girl put down the tray before her.

"*Bueno*," Pura smiled, showing very white teeth, and with a little courteous inclination of the head, left the room.

Venetia looked around the room as she lifted the silver coffee pot to pour out hot, fragrant coffee. Pale neutral walls and well cared for furniture gave a restful atmosphere of graciousness and charm. Gay rugs covered the floor and the bell rope beside her bed with its long golden tassel just asked to be pulled.

Later, she dressed prudently to be on the safe side in a crisply tailored cream silk blouse with a black velvet bow at the neck to match the one at the back of her tawny hair. Her slim black skirt looked demure and businesslike, she thought, pleased that her reflection in the dressing table mirror gave her the confidence she so badly needed to meet her new employer.

All the same her nervousness grew as she left her room and walked along the quiet corridor. I've done the right thing in coming here, she told herself shakenly. It's got to be. Then she began to relax as doors opened and heads peeped out. The grapevine had been busy. Apparently all the staff at the Villa Alicia had been alerted to the fact that the girl from Inglaterra had arrived. Venetia had to smile.

Doña Matilde was sitting beneath the shade of the sloping roof on the patio of the courtyard. Her hair shone blue-black as a raven's wing in the clear morning light and the jewelled comb in her hair twinkled in the sun catching the rings on her small hands. She turned her head swiftly at Venetia's approach, her look entirely Spanish. She spoke in English.

"You had a good night? But naturally your sleep would be one of exhaustion. However, you look rested and very pretty. Do sit down." She patted the seat beside her with a beringed hand. "No doubt you will feel strange at first, but you will soon become used to it. Have you any family?"

Venetia sat down, watching the small hands returning a monogrammed letter to its envelope.

She said, "I have a sister. No parents."

"That is sad for one so young." The liquid dark eyes lingered admiringly on the tawny hair shining in the sun like a web of fine silk. "Is your sister as pretty as you?"

27

"She is two years older than I and much prettier. She had Titian hair."

"And married, of course?"

Venetia shook her head. "No. Do Spanish girls marry so young?"

"No. The poor ones cannot afford to and the rich can take their time over choosing a husband."

Now that the conversation did not include Carolyn, Venetia began to breathe more freely. She said eagerly, "I was given to understand that some marriages in Spain were arranged by the parents. Forgive me for asking, but was yours?"

"Certainly." The black head lowered and Doña Matilde looked down sadly at the wedding ring on her hand. "I forgive you for asking. No, my marriage was not arranged. I do not believe there was ever a time when I did not love my Jaime. We grew up together." She sighed. "He died two years ago after twenty-seven years of wonderful happiness. Many people do not have one year, so my grief is tempered with the thought that I have so much to be thankful for. I have a daughter who is married and lives in Madrid and I have a son Federico who is here with me now. We left Madrid when James died and came to help Jorge run this estate."

"I am sorry, Doña Matilde, about your husband. You must miss him very much." Venetia spoke sincerely. The warmth of Doña Matilde's manner had done much to banish the strangeness, the brusqueness and the deliberate scrutiny, all part of this lovely country. Her eyes lingered on the peach-bloom skin with so few wrinkles. "You don't look old enough to have been married for twenty-seven years."

Doña Matilde laughed softly. "I assure you I have. Federico is twenty-six, my daughter twenty-four. Federico is not married. At the moment he is completely absorbed in running the estate. He was up very early this morning. You will meet him this evening at dinner. Now would you like to see over the house?"

Venetia walked through cool rooms of plane-washed walls and beautifully preserved furniture, ornate ceilings from which hung heavy brass lamps and lovely old paintings. The evidence of wealth lay in the exquisite embroidered tapestry on elegant chairs and inlaid cabinets, giving an atmosphere of cultured taste. The kitchen was a vast, spotlessly clean room dominated by a charcoal stove. The walls gleamed with pots and pans and the air was filled with the aroma of cooking and herbs.

Bypassing the apartments of Don Jorge, Doña Matilde said, "We are to take tea with my father this afternoon. He is much better after his bad chill which quite worried us at first. Now he is eager to begin work again, so he must be feeling better."

Venetia was tempted to tell her about changing places with Carolyn, but the moment passed and they returned once more to the courtyard to a mid-morning drink and tiny pastries.

Venetia had lunch with Doña Matilde, ice cold soup and a delicious salad of cold meats with fruit juice to drink, followed at the end of the meal with coffee. She could not sleep a wink during the afternoon siesta. Her thoughts were too much on the outcome of tea to be taken later that afternoon with Don Jorge. Tea had been laid in the dining room with the shutters closed to keep out the heat. Doña Matilde was waiting for her at the foot of the staircase, smiling reassuringly.

"Do not look so worried," she said. "My father is not an ogre. He will not eat you. Rather will he admire your fairness. Our Spanish males are adept at paying compliments to the fair sex. But we would have it no other way. You will like him – everyone does."

As they entered the dining room together, a tall sparse figure rose from a high-backed chair near the window. Don Jorge Moreno was a dignified, scholarly-looking man with a gentlemanly bearing. His features were typically Spanish, long, narrow and angular with a Van Dyke beard. His English was excellent and he gave the impression of a well read and learned man rich in experience and culture. He wore a velvet smoking jacket and a small cravat at his throat. He looked rather sallow after his recent illness, which was only to be expected, but he had the air of one fully recovered.

Doña Matilde, after greeting him and asking how he was, moved aside to introduce Venetia. He greeted her cordially with a twinkle in eyes so dark against the whiteness of his small beard.

He said, "Welcome to our country, Miss Mellor. I must apologize for being indisposed when you arrived, but you will understand that I deemed it wise to follow my doctor's advice and stay in bed for another day. Now I feel all the better for it."

"You are very wise, Don Jorge," Venetia replied, wondering if the neat beard was the instigator of the Spanish grandee's in his student days. She mentioned it as they sat down at the table.

Don Jorge smiled. "The young are so eager to look older and when they are old they want to look younger. I must agree that while the beard suited Ramón he is much handsomer without it. He had no weak chin to hide. Indeed he has the firm aquiline features of his father, who was also a very handsome man." He chuckled as he helped himself to cherry jam. "Now you are wondering if I have. That would be telling!"

Don Jorge's jocular manner made it easy for Venetia to relax and soon she was talking naturally about her childhood with Aunt Dorothy and the friendship with the Tamor boys next door. She dwelt only briefly on the event of the Ramón's entrance into her life, taking care to refer to him as the Señor Conde. Now was the time for her to tell Don Jorge about taking Carolyn's place, but somehow she could not work round to it, not with Doña Matilde listening so attentively to every word. Later perhaps when Don Jorge gave her a lead by talking about her former place of employment. But Don Jorge did not mention anything about her work in London. He was more concerned about her not being bored, buried as they were in the country.

"We shall only work in the mornings from nine until twelve," he told her, lighting a cheroot as they wandered outside to sit in the courtyard after tea. Doña Matilde had gone to see about dinner later that evening. "The afternoon is, as you know, spent in a siesta," he went on, seating her in one of the white cane chairs overlooking the courtyard before sitting down beside her. "The rest of the day will be yours to spend as you choose.

Dinner is not served until eight-thirty and is leisurely and long. We entertain friends and go out to dine with them. We should like you to dine with us every evening and also accompany us on our visits to friends – unless, of course, you have made other arrangements. You are young and will naturally seek the company of the young!" He smiled on her benignly. "You do not consider it too dull for you after London?"

"Goodness, no! I couldn't wait to come to all this warmth both of the sun and your people, Don Jorge. Everything is so wonderful. I like Doña Matilde very much."

"Ah yes. My daughter has not allowed the loss of her husband to embitter her in any way. She is like my nephew Ramón in that respect. She has courage and is grateful for past happiness."

Venetia nodded. "Yes, I remember the Span . . . the Señor Conde was very devoted to his father." She swallowed as her tongue tripped over the unfamiliar title. "He seems to be very sad and not a bit like he was at Tamor Hall."

Don Jorge studied the glowing end of his cheroot. "He had no responsibilities then. You know about his *novia*?"

"No."

"You will meet her in due course."

He said no more.

So the Spanish grandee had a fiancée. Venetia wondered about her as she prepared for dinner that evening. If Ramón had been betrothed in his youth he had waited a very long time to marry. But why? He was not the type of man to wait that long for a wife. Those black eyes, those slightly flaring nostrils, that mobile mouth all fused together gave the impression of a man capable of passion, impatient of delay and the will to have his own way regardless. After all, everything else had come his way, good looks, breeding, wealth and a healthy magnificent physique, so why not marriage? It was all very confusing.

Venetia slipped a demure little evening dress in blue silk over her tawny head, brushed her hair and used very little make-up. With white studs in her ears and a double link of white beads around her throat, she looked a perfectly suitable kind of person who would fit in with a Spanish household.

Venetia met no one on her way downstairs. As she crossed the hall, however, the sound of masculine voices came clearly from the open door of the library, a book-lined room, spacious and comfortable. She paused uncertainly by the doorway and instantly Ramón strode across the deep pile carpet to greet her.

Unsmiling as ever, he said politely, "Miss Mellór, good evening. You are down early. During my house parties at the Quinta Las Jacarandas, the ladies seldom arrive downstairs on time. I trust you are settling in, with no problems?"

Problems indeed! Venetia counted up to ten. "Yes, thanks. Everything is perfect," she murmured.

The blood rushed up beneath her clear skin. She was not too dumb to know what he meant. Well, she would explain to Don Jorge in her own time and not in the Spanish grandee's! He was needling her, of course, trying to make her angry.

He made the little bow which irritated her so much and she frowned a little when he said in the same flat polite tones, "As perfect as you appear to be yourself."

Venetia changed colour, opened her mouth to say something, then closed it again as his black eyes denied the compliment. She opened her mouth to speak again, but before she could say anything, Don Jorge, who was busy pouring wine at the huge carved table dominating the room, cut in.

"Come, do not be shy, Miss Mellor," he said jocularly. "We Spaniards delight in paying compliments. It is part of our language. Have an aperitif. It will take the blush of embarrassment from your cheek and bring a sparkle to your eyes which, I must admit, are sparkling already."

The glass of wine he held out was like a lifeline, Venetia thought, emerging from waves of anger to accept it.

"Sit down and make yourself comfortable."

Don Jorge waved her to a chair and turned to Ramón. "I would have you know, Ramón, that this young woman looked petrified upon meeting me this afternoon at tea. I am sure she was expecting some tyrant of a writer instead of a harmless old man."

Ramón accepted his wine with a lift of dark brows.

"Indeed?" he remarked after what appeared to Venetia to be a significant pause. "It is understandable, since neither of you know much about the other."

He had leaned nonchalantly against the heavy table, glass in hand, much too near to Venetia's chair for her comfort. She was waiting breathlessly for Don Jorge to reply when the rustle of silk drew her eyes to the doorway.

He had leaned nonchalantly against the heavy table, glass in hand, much too near to Venetia's chair for her comfort. She was waiting breathlessly for Don Jorge to reply when the rustle of silk drew her eyes to the doorway.

Doña Matilde entered the room accompanied by a young man of medium height who looked every inch a Spaniard. He was clean-shaven with sleek black hair, a rather sallow face and dark eyes which widened perceptively with admiration and delighted surprise when he saw her slender blue-clad figure.

After crossing swords, as it were, with Ramón, Venetia greeted Federico, Matilde's son, with more warmth than she would have done normally.

"*Mucho gusto*," she said, and blushed at the way he looked at her as though there was no one else in the room.

"I hope you will be very happy with us," he assured her with a white smile. "Maybe I will take up writing myself, then I can see you more often."

"You would never be happy working indoors," Doña Matilde said with a light laugh.

To which Federico replied quite goodhumouredly, "Ah, but look who I would have to type out my manuscripts!"

In the general laughter which followed Venetia looked up to see a cynical smile hovering around Ramón's well-cut lips. "You have made a conquest, Miss Mellor. Cheers." His eyes seemed to narrow dangerously.

He raised his glass and Venetia raised hers, feeling she had an ally in Federico. She would not be intimidated by a man who was once her friend and now appeared to be her implacable enemy. At the dinner table, seated between Federico and his mother, she began to feel that the evening would not be such an ordeal after all. During the course of the conversation she gathered that Ramón had been out with Federico around the estate all day discussing improvements and methods he used on his own land which were proving to be highly successful. He was explaining them now to Don Jorge, who apparently was very impressed. So also was Doña Matilde.

She noticed that he did not speak excitedly or rush his words. He spoke precisely and clearly in that deep cultured voice of his that, despite her determination to ignore him, sent prickles up her spine. She had never been so emotional before over any man, but in some strange way he prodded her into life and she was powerless against him. The thing was to play it cool. He did not reside in the house and she understood he was leaving early in the morning for his own home. While she felt at ease with the rest of the company, it was a transient ease which one glance from those black eyes could dispel in a moment.

No wonder their eyes were so dark, for these Spanish laid such emphasis on the messages they flashed out from those dark orbs – jealousy, passion, love, pride, dignity and something noble which Venetia found strangely endearing.

Venetia quivered suddenly from a slight inner tension, a longing to be accepted and at the time same to flee from she knew not what. She felt a confused foreboding of something fated, inescapable, final. Everything was in vibrant contrast – clear brilliant light, deep dark shadows, the scarlet lining of a black cloak, the flash of white teeth in a dark face, the sudden crack of clappers in the stillness as feet began to dance. All these things had a narcotic effect on the senses.

"You are very quiet," Federico whispered in her ear.

She started and smiled. "You must blame your country for that. Blame first impressions too, for I'm still reeling from them. Everything is so strange, so different. Here you are still clinging to your old code of life, yet richly enjoying every moment in a deep profound kind of way."

Federico's eyes crinkled at the corners from too much sun and outdoor life. "You like it?"

34

She nodded. "Oh yes, I like it. There's something in the air – a deep awareness of life around me, exciting, madly exhilarating." She laughed, quiet laughter which bubbled up inside her as she added, "And it doesn't mean the admiration in your eyes, Federico, so don't try to flirt with me."

He looked at her with an injured air. "You do not feel the vibrations inside you from my poor worshipping heart? I cannot believe it."

"You're talking nonsense!" she smiled.

"But, my angel, you have admitted to responding to influences around you. Why not mine?"

"Because I'm here to work and not to flirt," she answered firmly. "And I'm not your angel."

"But of course you are my angel," he insisted. "Shall I tell you what my first impressions of you were?" He bent his dark head and whispered in her ear under cover of the conversation. "I said to myself, Ah, a Botticelli angel come to reform me from my wicked ways. You sat there as though you had slid down a moonbeam and were waiting just for me."

Venetia chuckled. She would not have been natural not to enjoy the flattery, even though it was lightly meant and lightly given. It was idiotic, all the same, and it appeared that Ramón shared her opinion as she lowered her eyes hastily from his direct look in her direction.

It was after ten when dinner finally came to an end leaving Venetia feeling very sleepy. The change of air, the glass of wine she had taken before the meal and the little she had taken with it were having an effect. Several times she had to stifle a yawn and thought longingly of her bed. A phone call for Ramón to be taken in the library gave her the opportunity to leave the room in his absence. She knew he would have a word with her before she retired because he would leave before she was up the following morning. When they met again it would be easier to match his coolness, but now, bemused by good food, strong wine and a strange environment, she felt unequal to it.

Politely she excused herself on the grounds that she was very tired, and managed to give Federico the slip as he discussed the day's happenings on the estate with Don Jorge. Venetia had crossed the hall and was on her way up the staircase when her name was called, and her knuckles gleamed white as she gripped the balustrade and slowly turned around.

Ramón was striding from the direction of the library across the hall. He halted below her at the foot of the stair where the subdued lighting emphasised the blackness of his hair and the teak tan of his unsmiling face.

"Retiring so soon?" he said sardonically. "You must take the afternoon siesta more seriously, Miss Mellor. Only then will you find the Spanish nights enchanting. Federico will be very disappointed."

"Naturally," she answered, glad she was some distance away from his disturbing personality. She was dropping with fatigue, but would die rather than he should know.

He reached out a lean brown hand to rest it on the top of the carved post of the balustrade and she caught the gleam of a white cuff and the very masculine wrist watch.

"Allow me to give you a word of advice," he said. "Do not allow the flowery speeches you hear to turn your head. It is sometimes a Spaniard's way of being polite."

"But not yours."

The words were out before she was aware of having spoken. Strangely, she did not care. She saw the thinning of his mouth and the sudden gleam in the dark eyes.

"I, too, can use flowery speeches when there is a need for them. As a boy I had an English tutor, so naturally I am a little more reserved in consequence." His nostrils thinned. "I am merely warning you to take care. In a country of so much sun passions run high and what an Englishman would regard as purely a pass at him, a Spaniard would take it more seriously."

Venetia drew herself up to her full height, her tiredness for the moment forgotten. Her tawny eyes were weary but defiant. She gave him a long, hostile stare.

"If you've quite finished," she said, 'I'll continue on my way to my room. I'm very tired, but not too tired to take heed of your advice. In future I shall seek only Spaniards who've had an

36

English tutor. I might find them a little boring, but I shall be safe. Is that not so, Señor Conde? Good night."

Venetia was glad she was several feet above him, for at that moment he reminded her very much of the Moors, his ancestors. She could see the kerchief about his black head and the ear-rings gleaming in his ears.

The moment passed. He seemed about to say something, then thought better of it. Instead he bade her, "*Buenos noches*," then with an icy inclination of his head strode across the hall leaving Venetia to stare after him.

CHAPTER THREE

VENETIA was enchanted by the Spanish señoritas, and greatly admired their lustrous dark eyes and glossy black hair. Her own thick tawny hair above wide spaced eyes were her best feature, along with a slim, perfectly proportioned figure. Yet against the dark beauties who appeared to have been fed purely on peaches and grapes, her own looks seemed insipid. But she overlooked the fact that her mouth was sweetly curved with an enchanting sense of humour, her tawny eyes soft with gentleness and warmth of heart.

Don Jorge had given her the rest of the week to become acquainted with the countryside and encouraged her to explore a little and settle in before taking up her duties. Doña Matilde had taken her out to visit friends for tea. When the hour of siesta was over they would set out in Doña Matilde's own càr, which she drove herself very competently. Venetia grew familiar with the cool, dark interior of the houses where fingers of light, stiffly spread, lay on tiled floors and turned brass hanging lamps to gold. The older women looked very correct with black lace over their white hair, and sometimes a little matriarchal. On the whole, the younger ones were modest to a degree, decorative and utterly feminine. Yet despite their inhibitions nurtured by fond and often strict parents, Venetia felt they were capable of deep violent emotions of love and hate. It showed in the language of flashing black eyes communicating with each other.

On Sunday morning Venetia awoke to the chime of church bells. She got up quickly, washed and dressed and very soon, wearing a flower-sprigged cotton with white straw hat and white shoes, was adjusting her white shoulder bag to make her way downstairs. Doña Matilde waited for her in the hall and they went outside in the bright sunlight to where Don Jorge and Federico waited in a horse and trap. They were going to church.

As they jogged along the white dusty road with the pony proudly tossing the blue bobbles on his harness, Venetia decided that the only way to go to church was surely by horse and trap. The bells jingling on the harness mingled with goat bells as they passed the herds grazing in the fields and everywhere seemed so lighthearted and gay that she wanted to burst into song.

Today she saw another Federico, a quiet, more reserved young man who was inclined to take life more seriously at least one day of the week. After church they went home to breakfast and later, when Federico joined his grandfather in the library and Doña Matilde went to see about lunch, Venetia decided to take a walk.

With a book tucked under her arm, she set off happily beneath a blue sky. Everywhere light glittered, quivering from the walls of the villa to glance off the leaves of the fig trees, so that it was a relief to make for the shade of the drive and some sheltered place on a cool hill. The heat, which at first had made her feel languid, now gave her the feeling of a flower opening its petals to the sun. Beyond the formal gardens around the villa no hedges or walls broke the pattern of cultivated fields. Corn and vines stretched as far as the eye could see, punctuated by dark cypresses and occasional rows of silver olives.

Venetia strolled along the road to cut across fields seeking a path between the maize and making for a rise shaded by trees in the distance. She was steaming when she reached it to take off her hat and rake the flattened tawny hair away from her damp head. But it was cool beneath the trees and the view was really breathtaking, with the distant hills folding in the scene enchantingly. The slight murmur of the trees was very soothing and she sat down with a sigh of content and opened her book.

She returned to the villa feeling relaxed and uncaring, and gave herself ample time to change for lunch. In her happy preoccupation, Venetia failed to notice the car until the last moment. It pulled up ahead of her in the drive and the long figure of the Spanish grandee nonchalantly emerged. He stood waiting for her, taking in the smooth peach tan of her bare arms and throat. She had taken off her hat and pushed her hair behind her ears for coolness to reveal the lovely line of her cheek and jaw.

She felt his sharp dark eyes like needles probing for a sensitive spot and quivered with the knowledge that he had been constantly in her thoughts since their last meeting.

"Good morning, Miss Mellor. You look warm," he said, noting her deepening colour. "It is not wise to walk far in the heat."

Coolly he took the book from her and looked at the spine.

Instantly on the defensive, Venetia said stiffly, "I didn't go far, and I enjoy walking."

"All the same," dryly, "I am sure you would enjoy it more in the cool of the evening. How are you enjoying your stay in your temporary home?"

He was standing directly in her path, a fact which she resented, especially since she was wondering how temporary he was hoping her stay was going to be.

Militantly, she lifted her chin. "I like it very much, and I'm learning all the time."

The dark silky eyebrows were raised more than a fraction. His mouth twitched a little. "What about, the country or the people?"

"Both."

He returned the book. "So you study Spanish history. I could let you have a few books on the period Don Jorge's book is likely to cover."

Venetia teetered, trying to figure out whether he was testing her knowledge or offering to be friendly. The first was more than likely.

Imperceptibly, she withdrew to say coldly, "I'm sure I can borrow all I need from Don Jorge's library. Thanks all the same."

He inclined his head. "As you wish. A smattering of knowledge on the subject will not only serve to make your work more interesting, it will also please my uncle to know you are aware of what he is talking about."

"I'm sure it will."

Venetia saw the sudden tightening of his mouth. "I am not being patronizing. You and I are old acquaintances . . ."

"Ramón!" Doña Matilde's voice broke in delightedly.

"I thought I heard your car. You are staying to lunch, of course. This is a delightful surprise." Her warm smile included Venetia. "You look hot, Miss Mellor."

"I am. If you'll excuse me, I'd like to take a shower before lunch."

On reaching her room, Venetia sank down weakly into the nearest chair. That brief contact with Ramón, his re-entry into her life, had brought her feelings for him to the surface, feelings she had foolishly told herself she had under complete control. What an idiot she was to delude herself! Why, the very air hummed with the vibration of his presence in the villa. The very thought of meeting him again at lunch filled her with a sick nervousness.

As she looked back, her experience of men had been very limited. She had never been deeply disturbed by any young man of her acquaintance until now, not even when they had kissed her as they often had when taking her home from a date. Not one of them had made her feel terribly conscious of being a woman, nor had they altered her to their own masculinity as did Ramón Aldenez. Strangely enough he did not set himself out to charm women. He was so masculine, so charmingly nonchalant that his own unawareness of his charms did it for him. Her fingers curled in her moist palms as she recalled that she had not written to tell Carolyn that he was in Spain. Apart from a couple of cards about the weather, she had written no letter as yet.

Ramón's return to London would put things right where Carolyn was concerned. Was it possible that he was now on his way there and had called in to say goodbye? Well, at least that would be something.

Her arrival at the dining room was well timed. Doña Matilde met her at the door and they went in together. A neighbour of Don Jorge was there also, a dapper little man with a small moustache and an alert manner. The main topic of conversation between the men appeared to be about the improvements to Don Jorge's estate, while Doña Matilde asked about Venetia's recent walk and told her of similar interesting ones.

The anger had apparently gone from Ramón. He was now sometimes smiling, sometimes shrugging those wide shoulders in a tolerant, easy manner. His distinctive features were relaxed as he discussed some point of interest. Was business the only topic which was near to his heart, if he had a heart? Venetia doubted it.

Suddenly her heart went cold, for he was saying, "Why not come and stay at the Quinta for a short spell, Tio Jorge? You will have a better idea of what we are discussing if you see the estate. The sea air will do you good and pick you up. There is no reason why you should not begin to work on your book there. The library is at your disposal and there is plenty of room for yourself and Miss Mellor."

Venetia listened with dismay while they discussed it and her spirits fell to zero when Don Jorge accepted graciously. The lunch was over at last and everyone parted for the siesta, leaving Venetia feeling bewildered at the unexpected turn of events. She would miss Doña Matilde, but her work would take care of the mornings and living by the sea gave one endless opportunities to enjoy one's leisure. Feeling a little more cheerful, Venetia decided to take a short stroll in the garden before going to her room. The others, it seemed, had gone to see the next-door neighbour on his way.

She was crossing the hall when a figure filled the doorway in front of her and Ramón said smoothly, "No siesta, Miss Mellor?"

Oh dear, here we go again, she thought, and smiled brightly.

"I happen to be taking a short stroll in the garden in order to digest my lunch. Do you mind?"

"On the contrary, I will accompany you – that is if you do not mind." He slowed his long strides and walked beside her along a corridor and through a doorway which led outside to an inner courtyard. "You feel you will be happy here?" he asked casually.

Venetia's wide gaze was lifted to the dark saturnine features, loving the warm caress of the sun.

"The real difficulty is not settling down but tearing myself away when the time comes for me to go," she answered simply.

"Two years is a long time to stay away from familiar surroundings. We are what you would describe as country pumpkins here," he commented sardonically.

Venetia's giggle swung into a quiet throaty laugh. "The word is bumpkin."

She was feeling idiotically happy as he gazed down silently at her shining eyes, soft and luminous, and her lips tenderly curved. The intentness of his gaze made her rush on.

"You forget I was brought up in the country and I love it. I felt terrible when Carolyn and I went to live in London, though I've got used to it now."

"You mean you have become more attuned to city life?"

"I accept it."

He pushed his hands into his pockets and said carelessly, "You can always marry some country squire and go back again to your former life."

He had set his eyes in the distance to present an arrogant profile. Venetia gazed at the firm set of his jaw stamped with a rare strength of character which set him apart from other men of her acquaintance. That aura of mystery about him would be better left alone, she thought, and she wondered how on earth she had let herself be alone with him, much less walk with him in the garden.

Venetia assumed an attitude of calm as he stretched out a long arm above her head to set aside a trailing spray of scarlet flowers cascading from a pillar of vines in their path. The hot air was making her feel breathless, and his nearness did not help.

"It's an idea," she said lightly. "I must bear it in mind."

He steered her along shady walks, pausing at last by a low wall beyond which stretched a superb view of cultivated land against the backcloth of distant hills. Nonchalantly he leaned back against it and offered her his cigarette case. When she refused, he lighted one for himself and blew out a line of smoke heavenwards.

"What have you been doing with your time since you came?" he asked.

The tinkle of goat bells drew her attention to the outline of a herd on a distant rise accompanied by a shepherd. They appeared motionless in the heat. Only her heart appeared to be making any movement beneath the vast blue sky as it thumped against her ribs.

"Making myself familiar with the surroundings and meeting some of the local people."

A short silence followed while he digested this and Venetia toyed with the jagged edge of the stones which formed the top of the wall. She had an uneasy sense of having been taken for this short walk entirely for his own benefit. It would have helped had his manner been more friendly, but he seemed to have withdrawn into himself, almost as though he had forgotten she was there. Then he spoke.

"Tio Jorge is very impressed with you, Miss Mellor. He is a very shrewd and discerning man who does not enter lightly into friendships."

She bristled, sensing the note of censure in the deep voice. "Neither do I," she retorted, not attempting to hide her resentment of his attitude. "I like and respect Don Jorge very much and I'm looking forward to working with him."

"But you are not looking forward to going to the Quinta?"

Venetia gripped the rough stones. "Is it so surprising? You are obviously very much against my working for Don Jorge." Her chin lifted militantly. "Why?"

Her tawny eyes were perfectly steady, meeting his dark ones with a set look. Her face had gone pale and she waited.

He had relaxed against the low wall, his hands resting lightly on the top, the cigarette smouldering between long lean brown fingers; he was eyeing her coolly.

"I will be frank with you. I was very much against Tio Jorge employing a woman to type his memoirs."

Venetia stared at his dark inscrutable face with astonishment. "But why? You knew Carolyn?"

He inclined his head in agreement.

"Then why?" she insisted.

Bewilderedly, Venetia watched him inhale from his cigarette and send the smoke away from her in the opposite direction.

He looked strangely alien in that moment and very formidable with his El Greco face closed to any real probing.

"Tio Jorge had a young man at hand who would have been ideal, a young Spanish writer who possesses a good knowledge of the history involved and who also can speak half a dozen languages fluently."

The colour rose abruptly in her cheeks. "Then why didn't Don Jorge engage him?" she said stiffly.

He shrugged, a typically Spanish shrug. The black silky eyebrows lifted, but the dark eyes showed no emotion.

"I have no idea."

"I see." Venetia bit her lip. "You mean that if I had not taken my sister's place this writer would probably have been engaged in her place?"

"Probably," he answered laconically.

Venetia looked him full in the eyes. "It seems I must apologise for being a woman, since your disapproval seems to lie solely in the fact of my sex."

"It is none of my business."

"Then why mention it? I shall not let your uncle down and, upon reflection, I must add that Don Jorge must have had his reasons for not engaging this excellent young man." Her hands dropped from the wall and she clenched her fingers into her moist palms. But despite her determination to keep calm her voice quivered. "Now if you will excuse me, Don Jorge insist upon my taking a siesta after lunch. Good afternoon."

Venetia was no coward, but it took every ounce of courage to go smilingly with Don Jorge to Ramón's residence. It would have been easy to have told Don Jorge about her deception in taking her sister's place and go back to London. But she felt that to run away now after taking the plunge would be cowardly. The Spanish grandee had offered her a challenge. It was easy to see that he did not expect her to do the job with Don Jorge successfully. Well, she would show him!

Her packing was finished. She stood before her mirror in a smartly-cut navy tailored dress edged with white. Her hair had been swept into a neat chignon at the top of her head, smooth and very becoming. She would not need a hat in the car. The office dress, the neat hair-style gave her a formal appearance in keeping with her position, she decided, and was fastening a heavy chain bracelet to her wrist when Doña Matilde knocked on her door.

"You have finished packing, Miss Mellor?" The soft dark eyes rested briefly on the pigskin cases before appraising the smart demure dress and white accessories. "Pura said you did not require any help."

"Thanks, Doña Matilde, but I managed quite well. I haven't a great many clothes, and one needs less in a warm climate such as this."

"Federico would like a word with you before you go. He will see you in the library. He is there now if you are ready. I am sorry that your stay with us has been so short, but you will be back. The air will do my father good and you will enjoy it also."

Venetia smiled warmly. "I'm sure I will. I too am sorry to be leaving so soon. I've enjoyed being here so much. Please don't worry about your father – I'll look after him. And thanks for being so sweet."

She kissed the soft brown cheek and went lightly downstairs to the library. Federico was there, clad in his working clothes, well cut silk, open-necked shirt and breeches.

For some reason Venetia felt that he had been pacing the floor impatiently fretting the delay in his working day. But the frank admiration on his face as he hastened forward to greet her filled her with dismay. Her departure surely was not upsetting him so much? For a moment she was disturbed by the thought, then dismissed it as absurd and greeted him warmly.

"Am I keeping you from your duties, Don Federico?" she exclaimed. "I came immediately Doña Matilde told me."

"It is of no matter," he answered, holding her hand and smiling at her charmingly but sadly. "So you are leaving us, angel. We shall miss you, but you will return."

Venetia gently extricated her hand. "Yes, of course," she said awkwardly.

"Partings with friends are unpleasant." He folded his arms and looked at her very solemnly. "So of necessity we will make this a short one. But first a favour. I have a small packet which I would like you to deliver for me. Here it is."

He fetched a small, neat parcel from the table and handed it to her. She accepted it wonderingly. The concern in his voice was solely on behalf of his request – Venetia was sure of that. She waited.

"I want you to deliver it personally to Señorita Isabel Valrosa," he said sombrely.

"May one ask who she is?"

"The Señorita is Ramón's *novia*."

Venetia's eyes flew wide open. "Really? Shall I meet her?"

He nodded. "Perhaps not right away, but you will."

A frown creased her youthfully smooth forehead. "You look sad, Don Federico. Is anything wrong?"

A smile showed the startlingly white teeth. "Yes, my angel. You are going away, but do not forget me. My cousin Ramón entertains a great deal at the Quinta and you will enjoy yourself." Federico kissed her hand. "*Hasta la vista*, angel," he was saying as a tap came on the door and Ramón strode in.

For a brief moment his dark eyes flicked from one to the other. Federico straightened, and Ramón gave a faint supercilious bow in her direction. His voice was dangerously smooth.

"When you are ready, Miss Mellor. Don Jorge is in the car waiting. *Adios*, Federico."

With Don Jorge already seated in the back of the car, Venetia found herself seated beside his nephew who was obviously driving them to the Quinta himself. As the car slowly gathered speed, she tried to relax. The few days she had spent with Don Jorge and his family at the villa had made her feel at home but had not dimmed her delight in the ever-changing scenery around her.

She did not remark upon it because while her two companions appreciated all the grandeur filling their daily lives, they accepted it as a part of living. Without turning her head, Venetia was sure Don Jorge's head was already nodding in blissful

47

slumber, and the man beside her was concentrating on his driving in a way which waved aside any conversation. Was this visit more than an act of kindness to Don Jorge? Was it going to prove embarrassing or worse job-wise? Teetering in a state of anti-climax, Venetia asked herself what was the worst that could happen. Don Jorge could do no more than fire her. In that case she would return to London and look out for a suitable job. There were heaps of jobs going begging for office staff, hosts of opportunities. One only had to find the right one.

Gradually her anxiety receded, leaving her free to soak herself in the passing scenery, the quaint windmills, the pale colour-washed houses, the mountains huddled together like a herd of elephants ranging from smoky blue to ochre. The sky was a vast ceiling of blue shimmering heat where movement was slow. A great bird with a vast wing-span moved lethargically across the blue, making for the mountains they were now tossing behind them.

Hard to believe that London was now in the cruel grip of a merciless February while here the sun, gaining more heat with the day, smiled down on irrigated fields of maize, eucalyptus and olive groves. Venetia sat up with interest when they passed a mountain stream where women were busy washing clothes. Ramón tossed her an amused glance and she felt bound to remark upon it.

"How refreshingly clear and sparkling the water looks," she commented. "I suppose there's no pollution in these parts?"

"Very little. Things are quiet at the moment, with late spring and early summer the busiest times. By then beans are ready for picking and potatoes, eggplants and melons are sown. Wheat is harvested to make room for Indian corn, lentils and so on."

Listening to the deep cadence of his voice, Venetia began to sag a little with fatigue. Her head had begun to feel too heavy for her slender neck and it began to nod. The car swerving around sharply wakened her. She had slipped sideways in her seat and her head rested by Ramón's shoulder. Embarrassment shook the last remnants of sleep from her brain and she sat upright to smooth back her hair with an unsteady hand.

The car was travelling smoothly and opulently along a road lined with enormous old trees between orchards and vineyards. There was a salty tang in the air cool with the fragrance of orange and lemon trees. Bougainvillea, magney and prickly pear rioted in colour against the background of brown and green earth and shimmering blue sky. To their left Venetia glimpsed dazzling views of the sea between the trees while on their right an enormous thick stone wall covered with a thick profusion of purple creepers seemed to go on and on.

The beautiful wrought iron gates were open and they slid between massive pillars to cruise along a drive of superb tamarinds, stately cedars and pines. Then it was no longer a road but a garden brilliant with flowering shrubs, and violent splashes of exotic blooms drooping over green lawns. The place lay in sleepy silence except for the twitter of birds. And there it was like a crown edged by the silvery blue cloak of the bay, the Quinta Las Jacarandas.

Deep awnings and closed shutters protected windows and loggias from the sun and a series of Moorish arches formed a ground floor façade to give a unique sobriety and singular elegance to the towering stone pile. The car turned smoothly into a courtyard where, on a floor of Renaissance marble, rotund earthenware jars overflowed with petunias, fuchsias and scarlet geraniums. In the centre a marble fountain of graceful nymphs supported a rainbow spray of showering rain.

As Ramón helped Venetia from the car an elderly woman in a demure black dress, her hair taken back in a knot at the nape of her neck, came from the shadows of a doorway to greet them.

"*Buenos dias*," Ramón said as he helped Don Jorge from the car. "Miss Mellor, my housekeeper, Doña Uraca." Then he turned as several more of the staff joined them. "Your maid, Miss Mellor, Rosa, who will escort you to your rooms."

A girl stepped forward from the small procession of black-dressed people who had come forward to be introduced before they separated to their various duties. Rosa was a pretty girl in her teens with ripe dark looks and a provocative figure. She walked with the grace of a dancer and her dark eloquent eyes spoke more forcefully than her tongue ever could.

"*Buenos días, señorita,*" she said softly in pleasant tones, and led the way indoors.

Still bemused by all the grandeur, Venetia was inclined to giggle as, with the maid, she headed the procession indoors. As she walked across a hall of honey gold tiles she was conscious of rich tapestry-covered walls and beautifully carved furniture against white walls. There was an air of muted wealth, of culture, creating a perfect setting for gracious living.

The house was quiet when Venetia went downstairs for dinner that evening. She had sent Rosa away after she had run her bath and put out the simple lace evening dress with a heart-shaped neckline and long sleeves. The little evening bag on her wrist matched the slippers peeping beneath the full skirt. Nervously she had surveyed herself in the mirror in her room and had felt reassured by her demure appearance.

In the hall she paused to peep through the nearest archway into a room. It was obviously the dining room with a long dark gleaming table set with lace mats, gleaming cutlery and beautiful flower arrangements. The furniture, dark but richly glowing, the low couches, the crystal glass candelabra, the long sideboard gleaming with silver dishes looked opulent but not austere.

Venetia entered the room silently on the thick carpet and walked to the sideboard to pick up a serviette from a small pile set ready. In one corner was embroidered the family crest with the words she had noticed over the entrance on arriving. *Todo o nada.* All or nothing. She quivered, sensing the Moorish influence all around her. It was there following her as she moved swiftly across the room and into the hall as though to flee from something which was not of her world.

The next archway led into a sitting room where Ramón was standing at a gold and glass cabinet filled with a selection of incredibly sparkling bottles. He turned as she entered and smiled, that charming rare smile which, for her, seldom reached those dark compelling eyes.

"Come in," he said. "I am not going to eat you, although I shall welcome dinner. I trust your appetite, like mine, has not been impaired by the long and tiring journey."

His air of comfortable elegance, of clothes donned nonchalantly and worn with his own inimitable style of grace, caught at her heart. There was a drift of after-shave lotion as she drew near enough to accept her drink and her breath caught in her throat. Again there was that wild urge to escape from she knew not what. But it was too late. The sight of his dark head slightly inclined as he poured out a second glass of wine for himself sent the tremors of desire so shatteringly through her entire being that she had to make for the nearest chair on legs suddenly gone weak.

The violence of her emotions robbed her of breath, and she knew that for good or ill she was in love and would be until the day she died. That first exciting interest he had evoked in her had grown and strengthened beyond all proportion, making her only too sure that the next two years would be spent in the bitter-sweet agony of unrequited love. Feverishly, she hoped they would not be dining alone and longed for Don Jorge to put in an appearance.

He had moved with his drink to the fireplace to look down on her and raise his glass with that easy, relaxed air of camaraderie which he could summon at will.

"Cheers," he said.

Venetia murmured a reply and sipped her sherry, only to hear his next words putting an end to her hopes.

"Don Jorge will not be dining with us this evening. He is tired and will be retiring early. I am hoping his stay at the Quinta will see him much improved in health. I trust you are not too fatigued yourself."

He sounded more precise and formal, if that were possible. The journey had obviously done nothing to impair his wonderful physique. He had tossed it off as he was tossing off his drink.

She said, "It was a long journey, but I enjoyed every moment until I went to sleep." Her mouth curved and she was valiantly trying to subdue the wave of hot colour mounting to her cheeks at the thought of her head on his shoulder when she had wakened. "The scenery was breathtaking – all those mountains!"

The signet ring on his finger caught the light as he put down his glass.

"You will see mountains wherever you go in Spain. More wine?"

Venetia refused politely and because she felt it was expected of her began to make casual conversation. "Your family motto, Señor Conde – all or nothing. I find it rather sweeping." As the black silky eyebrows drew together in a frown she hurried on, "I mean, it's so definite, and a little frightening."

"Frightening?" The dark eyes narrowed slightly as he went on with faint satire. "We have come a long way from your Shakespeare's *Othello*, Miss Mellor."

"Yet I would say your family motto has remained the same through the centuries. You must admit that it sounds . . . fatalistic."

He shrugged contemptuously. "You would prefer half measures? They are for the weak."

Venetia smiled. She could not help it. "Please, don't misunderstand, but I have to smile because at the moment with your eyes flashing you look very much like those Moors of long ago." She put her head on one side impishly and studied his dark face. "Yes, a pair of ear-rings and perhaps a red kerchief around the head."

The flashing eyes captured her tawny ones. The culture of generations had given them an enigmatic look, but the fire flamed beneath the surface and she quivered. He answered without moving a muscle.

"I think, Miss Mellor, that you should regard yourself as being extremely fortunate that I have neither ear-rings nor a red kerchief."

Suddenly her heart gave a leap of pure terror as the devil dancing briefly in his eyes cornered the little imps dancing in her own. It was like being on the big dipper at a fair, terrifying yet at the same time exhilarating.

Really the wine was stronger than she could have ever imagined, for she went on to ask him what to her was a dangerous and leading question.

"I should like to ask you something concerning my sister. Would you have been happier if Carolyn had come here as arranged instead of myself?"

The moment the words were spoken, Venetia was regretting them, for a shutter came down on his face. Slowly he drew himself up to his six foot odd and in doing so seemed to tower menacingly above her.

His voice was on ice. "You are in my house at my invitation. I admit I rather hoped things would be different, but that is no matter."

Her soft lips tightened. He had evaded her question as she had expected he would. "But wasn't that rather rash of you – rubbing the salt in the wound, as it were?"

His voice was as smooth as cream. "How aptly you put it! In the circumstances it makes little or no difference whether your sister came or you."

There was a short embarrassed silence until Venetia, goaded by his arrogant manner, said deliberately, "I find it hard to believe that a man with the blood of Moors in his veins should be so averse to feminine company. I would have said you are far too masculine to lead a celibate life."

The dark eyes were quickly masked, the well cut lips purely cynical.

"You would be right, Miss Mellor. I would not be a normal man with a normal man's desires had I not lived a full life. I have had my moments, but they have passed with time. Satisfied?"

Venetia coloured hotly. She sobered, wondering what had got into her.

"I'm sorry," she apologised with a touching air of youthful dignity which sat lightly on her slender charm. "I'm afraid I went far beyond my position here to broach so personal a subject. Please forgive me."

She raised her eyes appealingly to his face, but he was looking towards the door as a knock requested admittance. The door opened at his command and a most enchanting young woman entered in a gown of black satin and lace with a flower in her

53

raven locks. She was accompanied by an elderly woman who hung back near the door as though expecting to be dismissed.

Venetia saw a small face with winged brows, dark eyes and a small, beautifully modelled mouth. But it was the eyes which held Venetia; they were vacant. It was the face of a doll, emotionless and innocent. There was a look of distinction about the carriage of the small head, the lovely lines of her slender body, the tilt of her chin and the silky eyebrows, despite the extraordinary expression.

"You may go, Luisa," Ramón commanded, as he strode forward to greet the newcomer. Then he had taken the small hands and was drawing her across the room. "Miss Mellor," he said gravely, "may I introduce you to my *novia*, Señorita Isabel Valrosa?"

The meal progressed through its innumerable courses. Venetia, completely bewitched by the lovely Isabel, touched her lips to wine, tasted a little of each serving and smiled at the girl, who appeared to be around her own age. She noticed that Ramón watched over his *novia* most of the time. It was he who put the food on her plate from the manservant's hand, he who replenished her wine glass with a little more wine and he who decided when she had eaten enough.

Gradually the awful truth dawned upon Venetia. This beautiful young woman who looked as though she had been fed entirely on peaches and cream was impaired mentally. But how? It must be something which had happened since they had become engaged, for he would hardly have committed himself to her otherwise. A lump rose in her throat at his tolerance and infinite gentleness.

It was ten o'clock when Luisa came to collect her charge and Venetia watched them go, shaken by the awful tragedy to one so young. Her host had lit a cigar and she looked at him covertly. He looked immensely strong and vital, but the strength was underlain by fatigue. It occurred to her that he was far too lean. The dark eyes beneath the straight brows were fathomless pools in which one could blissfully drown if . . . Venetia pulled

54

up her thoughts with a jerk to find him studying her.

"You are very quiet, Miss Mellor. Did you enjoy your meal?" he asked, tapping the ash from his cigar into an ashtray on the table.

"I enjoyed it very much, thank you," she replied quietly.

"You are tired?"

"A little," she admitted.

"But not too tired to take a short stroll in the garden before going to bed?"

He had stubbed out his cigar as he spoke and was on his feet to pull the bell rope and summon a servant to fetch a wrap from her room. Soon they were crossing the courtyard lighted by lanterns hung on the walls and he was holding her elbow in a light grip which made her quiver inwardly. The air was sweetly narcotic with the perfume of flowers when, leaving the courtyard, they walked across lawns to a pathway among the well laid out grounds.

For a while neither of them spoke, being content to enjoy the beauty of the night. But Venetia was thinking of the tragic Isabel and wondered if Ramón was thinking of her too. Poor Carolyn! It seemed after all that he was not interested in her to the extent that she was interested in him. It was a relief to know this, because had he liked her sister then her own conduct in not letting Carolyn know that he was here would have been treacherous and disloyal.

In the light of the newly risen moon, now past its first quarter, flowers glimmered like waxen blossoms, and as they strolled towards the trees the song of the nightingale rose softly on the clear night air. Enchanted, Venetia forgot everything but the clear sweet notes coming from the tiny throat, and the man beside her was part of it. The half moon was throwing enough light to show them clearly to each other and Venetia raised glowing eyes to the face above her as the last notes of the bird died away.

"Wasn't it divine?" she whispered, still under the spell of the heavenly notes.

"Perfect," he agreed, looking intently down into her face.

"I find it delightfully refreshing to gaze upon the face of a happy woman. You are fond of nature, Miss Mellor. So many women these days tend to go for all the material things in life and miss the worthwhile things which make life worth living. You have that rare quality that appreciates simple joys. That small chuckle you have bubbles from the heart and your compassion is boundless. I noticed it this evening at dinner."

"Did you?" she replied bewilderedly.

"I did not enlighten you about my *novia*, as I wanted to see your reaction when you met her. So many regard her as some strange object and act accordingly. You behaved naturally with her, and I wish to thank you."

"But surely it's I who should be thanking you for giving me the pleasure of staying in this lovely Eden. I've never been in such idyllic surroundings, where time is of no account and only real things matter."

Venetia was shaken by a host of different emotions. She wanted to laugh because she was gloriously happy and she wanted to cry at the new note in his voice. That he, her Spanish grandee, should be humble squeezed tears from her heart.

Now it was his turn to chuckle softly in the darkness. "So the Quinta Las Jacarandas is in the Garden of Eden! How very apt, since I am not to touch the forbidden fruit."

His laugh had become bitter. Venetia wanted to put out a gentle hand to soothe the bitter lines she knew were about his mouth.

"But you have so much to recompense you in your garden while you wait for ultimate happiness. You have the richness of your inheritance – and I don't mean money," she assured him warmly.

"What do you mean?" he asked softly, and there was a note in his voice which brought the small quiver of excitement to riot again in her veins.

"I mean all the loveliness preserved through generations of change elsewhere. Unlike us, you've had the good sense not to change the character and culture of your race. It's all intact, along with all the graciousness and nobility which makes us all more human. I wonder that you would ever wish to leave it."

"You would not wish to leave it, Miss Mellor? First impressions can cloud one's judgement. I am afraid in time my garden of Eden will begin to pall. I shall ask you again when your sojourn here is ended."

The answer will be the same, her heart cried, and because the thought of leaving him hurt her so much she forgot to be discreet.

"You don't realize how lucky you are, do you?" she cried.

"Lucky?" he echoed, then added ironically, "How would you define the word lucky, Miss Mellor?"

He had turned to take a path leading back to the Quinta and she walked with him, feeling that it would be safer for her indoors away from a conversation rapidly getting out of hand.

"You are a good definition of it. You have everything life can offer except marriage," she said desperately.

"You consider this important?" dryly.

"Of course it is. Here you have this gorgeous *quinta*, the ideal place to bring up a family to carry on your name. The greatest blessing on this earth is to be loved for yourself, and that's what you would be by your family."

There was a pause while he appeared to digest this. "You have strong views on the subject of marriage. I find this strange since you are not married yourself. You are . . . twenty-two years of age, are you not? Why are you not married?"

"Because I've been waiting to meet the man I can love above all others. I've had light affairs, nothing serious or intimate."

"And when you meet this man you will live with him first in order to discover if you are compatible. That is the favourite trend in your country, is it not?"

"You're talking about the minority," Venetia said furiously. "Quite a number of my friends have morals and stick to them. Also I would have you know that neither my sister nor I have slept around with anyone!"

They had entered the courtyard and he looked down at her flashing tawny eyes in the light of the lanterns.

He said quietly, "It seems I owe you an apology, Miss

Mellor. I am not so narrow-minded as to judge every person the same."

"I should hope not," Venetia replied with spirit. "I bet there are one or two passions smouldering around here under cover. Rosa, my maid, is a provocative minx if ever I saw one."

"Rosa?" He frowned. The next moment he was throwing back his head and laughing. In the light of the lanterns his teeth were a bar of whiteness in his tanned face and something caught at her heart. "Ah yes. Now you come to mention it, Rosa is . . . er . . . provocative."

Venetia gazed up at him in astonishment. "You mean to say you haven't noticed it particularly?"

The dark eyes were twinkling down at her. Really they were most expressive as he said sardonically, "The fact had not escaped me. After all, I am a man. On the other hand, I was not impressed by it since I am not in the habit of ogling my staff. I also have a code which I live up to, Miss Mellor. A man in my position has to set an example."

"I appreciate that," she conceded, and fell silent, knowing she had already said too much.

"Also," he added as he guided her to a seat by a brazier beneath the arched façade of the patio, "Rosa's experience with men is only in her mind. One has only to glance once at her eyes to know that she is entirely innocent. So it is with you, Miss Mellor. An experienced man can tell by the eyes of any woman the purity of her soul." He seated her and stood a few feet away with his back against a marble pillar. "You have that untouched look of purity which used to shine in the eyes of my *novia*. I would like to tell you about her."

He turned slightly to gaze out into the night, and the quiet perfection of his clothes struck her anew. He really was beautifully made, she thought, strong and well built with those wide shoulders and lean hips and that clear cut profile poised so arrogantly.

"She was an only child. Her parents and mine were lifelong friends. It had always been their wish that Isabel and I should marry one day because of that friendship. She was sweet and

58

adorable and I saw no reason why I should not bow to the wishes of my parents and marry her. Four years ago, on her eighteenth birthday, we became betrothed. The following morning Isabel went into her mother's room to discover her dead. Her husband had risen early and she must have had a heart attack soon after he left the room. Isabel rushed from the room in a state of shock, tripped on the top step of the stairs and plunged to the bottom, striking her head on the banisters as she fell. When they picked her up she could not speak and has never spoken since. She also has the mentality of a child."

"Oh dear, how terrible!" Venetia said in a shocked whisper.

He went on, "It was impossible for us to marry. So I wait in the hope that she will eventually regain everything she has lost." He straightened as though to ease the burden on his shoulders and smiled down at her in the golden light. The smile did not reach his eyes. "My *novia* lives in a villa in the grounds here. It would please me greatly if you would call on her occasionally for tea during your hours off duty."

Venetia hesitated. This was something she had not foreseen. What a blow to Carolyn to hear that the Spanish grandee was engaged to someone he could not very well free himself from honourably. Poor Isabel!

Her compassion shone in her clear eyes. "I'll be happy to call on her. I'll do anything that I can. You have only to ask me."

"*Gracias*, you are very kind."

He spoke with real feeling, the dark eyes regarding her filled with a curious light. To her annoyance, her face flamed hotly.

"Not at all. And now if you'll excuse me –" Venetia rose to her feet feeling the need for her bed. "Good night, Señor Conde."

"*Buenas noches*, Miss Mellor. Sleep well."

She walked indoors knowing he was watching her from the doorway, and found no satisfaction in the knowledge.

CHAPTER FOUR

"THAT will be all for today, Miss Mellor. Not a bad morning's work, I would say."

Don Jorge removed his spectacles and smiled across at Venetia, well pleased. It was their first morning at work on the book. The library, being both useful for reference books and one of the coolest rooms in the Quinta, had been allotted to them. Don Jorge had sat at the huge carved table where Ramón carried out his business of the estate.

Venetia rose from her typewriter and walked across the room to place the sheets of paper before him. She looked neat and efficient with the lightest of make-up on her face. The one light touch was the bow of black velvet ribbon pinned on the back of her hair to match the black, pencil-slim skirt and tiny black bow on the smart tailored cream silk blouse.

At nine o'clock precisely that morning she had tapped on the door of the library, to be greeted by Don Jorge, who had asked if she had slept well with a smile which had put her immediately at her ease.

"Here is the introduction to my book, Miss Mellor," he had said, passing the closely written pages across the huge table to her. "It is written in English and is to be sent to an English publisher. I would appreciate it if you would comment on anything you do not understand, also to query any phrase which you might consider as being too Spanish. We can then proceed to moderate it." His smile had been very kind. "And, Miss Mellor, do not be afraid to ask questions, they are more easily handled than mistakes."

They had worked together for three hours with a break for mid-morning chocolate and Venetia had enjoyed every moment. Don Jorge, she had discovered, was a man of extraordinary ability who could read, write and speak English with an admirable elegance, pronouncing his words clearly with a knowledge of an extremely large vocabulary.

They had lunch together, with Ramón conspicuously absent. Venetia knew a sense of relief, for she felt a breathing space was necessary before they met again. In the dimness of the dining room with its closed window shutters his presence was almost palpable. Where was he now? Had he gone back to London? Don Jorge did not mention him during lunch and gave her no excuse to do so. So, after lunch, she went to her room, deciding to write to Carolyn before she took her short siesta.

She was sealing the letter when the maid Rosa appeared, all smiles.

"Is there anything you require, Miss Mellor?" she enquired.

Venetia shook her head. "Nothing, thanks, Rosa. I shall go to post a letter and explore a little when I've taken my siesta."

"Explore?" Rosa's smooth forehead wrinkled, the winged eyebrows lifted.

Venetia laughed. "Take a walk to the village and perhaps bathe in the sea. In short, find my way about."

Rosa nodded comprehendingly. "Ah yes, the beach is delightful, and there are some very sheltered coves from the sun."

The dark eyes looked at her completely innocently before she walked provocatively from the room. Recalling Ramón's comments, Venetia pursed her lips thoughtfully, then laughed joyously as she put the letter down and lay on her bed. The rest of the day was her own to do as she liked. What pure bliss! She closed her eyes.

Refreshed by the siesta and a quick shower, she set forth in a cool cotton sun-dress and a large shady hat to walk to the village to post Carolyn's letter. The warmth of the sun and the ex-hilarating air filled her with a sense of wellbeing. It was possible to see the village from the grounds of the Quinta. Snuggled in a hollow, it lay peacefully beneath a succession of terraces of small farms while immediately below lay the sea washing languidly against white, clean beaches. All around the coastline as far as Venetia could see was unspoiled natural country. Ramón's estate was obviously a large one where no developers had yet invaded.

61

Taking a path which looked like leading down to the beach, Venetia walked lightly in roped sandals. Five minutes later she was on the shore and discovered to her delight that it was possible to walk along it to the village, much better than along the dusty roads where mule carts kicked up the choking white dust.

In the village, she strolled through narrow twisting cobbled streets in search of the post office. She looked up at the grilled windows of ochre-roofed houses where the delicate structure of ironwork was half hidden by trailing blue and purple bougainvillea and morning glory and listened to the mournful singing of a housewife busy with her chores. The air was a mixture of wine, oil, charcoal and sea. In the square by the fountain two little girls posed demurely in their white confirmation dresses for their photographs. Here the air was impregnated with the scent of orange trees which gave shade to seats where the old men sat wrinkled as walnuts over their smelly old pipes. As Venetia made her way to the post office with its vantage point overlooking the square, she politely ignored the bold glances of wickedly handsome young Spaniards with black greased hair and curling moustaches.

The woman at the counter was dressed in rusty black with a black kerchief over her hair. Her age, Venetia decided, was uncertain, for while her skin had the wrinkled texture of a middle-aged woman, her body had the lissom grace of a dancer. She had very fine dark eyes with a lurking sense of humour behind them.

Everyone in the village was interested in the young woman from Inglaterra who was staying at the Quinta; she volunteered in English, explaining that she had been in service with an English family residing in Madrid before her marriage. She knew the Señor Conde's *novia* very well, having met her in Madrid. Everyone had been shocked at the tragedy of her mother's death and all the village were so sorry for the Señor Conde, who was so very *simpatico* and so very, very *atractivo*. She passed over Venetia's stamps with much shaking of the head. So sad. Everybody adored the Señor Conde.

The interior of the little shops was stifling in the heat and Venetia did not linger over her few purchases. At the last shop in the high street, she paused to admire a few articles of beaten silver displayed on velvet in the window. The name over the shop was Fadrigo. It was the little flamenco doll which lured her inside. Isabel would love it, she was sure.

When her eyes became accustomed to the dimness after the brightness of outdoors, she saw a young man seated at a table behind the counter making the jewellery displayed in the window. He had the face of an artist, sensitive, dreamy and sensual. He rose at her entrance and came to the counter.

Aged around thirty, he had ridiculously long eyelashes and dark, melancholy eyes which lighted up with such blatant admiration of her slim fairness that she blushed hotly. Then, putting it down to his sales technique, she asked for the flamenco doll in the window. Before he produced it he picked up several pieces of jewellery from his work table, holding them up to catch the light with little bows, elaborate flourishes and ecstatic murmurings.

"*Hermosa, hermosa,*" his hoarse voice crooned, while he put his head on one side and lifted a knowing eyebrow for her approval.

Venetia, teetering on the edge of laughter at his provocative moves, gazed longingly at an exquisite necklace of twining leaves and stones, knew it would be far more than she could afford and asked again in halting Spanish for the doll.

He produced it at last after several soulful glances of disappointment from his melting eyes and she picked it up.

"I'll take it," she said, her eyes straying inadvertently again to the necklace.

Instantly he pounced upon it. "You like it?" The black eyes glowed. "I make it for a beautiful woman. For you."

She laughed at his absurdity. "It is very beautiful and I like it very much, but I can't afford it."

His face lighted up with the expression of a man to whom praise of his work meant more to him than money.

"Like me, Fadrigo, you appreciate beauty, English miss,

63

so you shall have it. Shall I tell you something?" He leaned earnestly over the counter and her gaze became entangled in the marvellously long eyelashes. "Always when a pretty woman from Inglaterra comes into my shop I tell myself, Fadrigo, you must learn more English. And what do I do?" The expressive shrug was accompanied by a display of the palms of his hands. "I become engrossed in my work and forget." Another shrug, this time accompanied by a grimace. "Spanish, that is easy, for it is spoken as it is written. English takes longer, much longer."

Venetia said, "But you speak English beautifully. I wish I could speak Spanish half so well."

"Your Spanish, *senorita*, is of the highest quality. The accent is superb."

He brought the tips of his fingers together, kissed them and waved the kiss in the air. Venetia blushed again, knowing he could be right since Ramón had been her teacher. Ten minutes of the exchange of languages followed. He would whisper a few words in Spanish across the counter, Venetia would savour them with a nod and would then translate them into English. At this he would shake his head, sigh heavily and give her a look of admiration. "*Hermosa*, a superb accent," he said, raising those melting eyes to the ceiling.

When Venetia eventually left the shop she carried the doll and the necklace. The latter had been forced upon her as a payment for the lessons in English. She had refused to accept it as a gift and after much argument Fadrigo had priced it at a ridiculously low figure. She had given him more than he had asked, but even then it was well below the worth of the necklace.

Upon returning to the grounds of the Quinta, she began to look around for the villa where Isabel Valrosa lived. Everything was quiet. Even the birds seemed to be enjoying a long siesta. Venetia had the sensation of having stepped from all the activity of the earth to enter a charmed and beautiful place where people lived as noiselessly as flowers beneath the caressing warmth of the sun. There seemed to be no sign of life and instinctively one was prepared to hold the breath and walk on tiptoe.

Wide green velvet lawns stretched between the orange, pinks, lemon-yellows and deep purples of fruit trees and flowers, fountains rainbow-hued dripped over nymphs and Aphrodites and cloistered walks led on and on.

And suddenly there it was, embowered within a profusion of flowers, secure against curiosity and intrusion. Venetia gazed at the long white building with its paved patio, blue shutters and open door flanked by rotund flower-filled jars. So this was where Isabel lived.

Venetia's mouth curved sweetly as she took in every detail. A Sleeping Beauty's palace with the handsome prince just around the corner, she thought wryly, and found herself envying the tragic Isabel who had his love. Her fingers closed around the doll. She was in no fit state to pay a visit until she had taken a shower and changed her dusty dress for a clean one. Maybe when she returned there would be some life about the place.

She had showered and changed into a dress of pale blue cotton and fastened the necklace of intricately designed silver leaves and flowers around her slim throat. Her hair had been swept up into a smooth chignon and the effect was one of cool elegance. Collecting the doll and Federico's parcel, she left the room.

The hot silence was dreamlike and nothing stirred except the butterflies and bees among the blossom when Venetia went along the cloistered walk to the villa. The tranced atmosphere was narcotic in the stillness and the sunlight dazzled the eyes as the walk ended and she was staring once more at the little villa. Before her on the loggia, Isabel sat with Luisa. For several moments Venetia stood to watch the girl weaving a chain of small yellow flowers. Poor Isabel! She was in the position of a child who could be told to run away and play, except that Luisa was there to wait upon her and amuse her all day. She was as lovely as any fairy tale princess, Venetia thought, with the sun shining on the black satin of her hair. Her small head was poised on her slim neck like a flower as she bent over the necklace she was weaving. Was she on the borderline of awakening or was she doomed forever to remain as she was? Venetia's heart beat a little faster at the thought of the Spanish grandee striding towards her to carry her away to the heights of bliss. This was the place, the ideal spot for lovers' meeting, but Venetia was learning that the heart can know torture even in the most beautiful surroundings.

Luisa saw her first and came towards her with a light tread despite her plumpness. She had obviously been told to expect the young woman from Inglaterra by the Señor Conde, for her dark eyes showed no surprise, merely a courteous welcome.

Venetia spoke first. "I trust I'm not intruding, Luisa, but I have presents for Señorita Isabel. One is from Señor Federico Moreno from Santa Marta. The other is from me."

Luisa nodded comprehendingly. "*Gracias*, Miss Mellor, you are very kind. Will you give the gifts to the Señorita while I go to the kitchen? You will take tea with her?"

Venetia nodded. "I would like that very much."

Luisa, after saying a few quick words to Isabel, motioned for Venetia to sit down in one of the white cane upholstered chairs and left them. Isabel, who had dropped the chain of flowers on her knee, took the two packages from Venetia with no change of expression. Even the name of Federico failed to bring forth any spark in the vacant black eyes. She was evidently used to receiving gifts, for her small hands tore away the paper and she threw it to the ground with the inconsequence of a child.

Federico's present was a crystal ball which, when turned, revealed lovely coloured designs of every shape and colour. Isabel looked at it fascinated for quite a while. Then, to Venetia's amusement, she handed it to her while she undid the wrapping from the doll. If Federico's present had given her joy the little flamenco doll sent her into pure delight. She cooed over it softly, her fingers touching the flounced dress and tiny feet almost reverently.

When Luisa came with the tea tray, she held it up to show her, making the same noise in her throat which never dissolved into words. Venetia held the crystal between her hands, wishing it was indeed something magic in which she could read Isabel's future. But the colours only mocked and she put it down on the table Luisa had brought near to spread the tea.

Venetia enjoyed the tea. Luisa sat by knitting and talking to her while Isabel ate little, being entirely absorbed in her presents. The chain of yellow flowers had been wrapped around the flamenco doll and Isabel went to pick more from the garden. On her return, she made more chains which she wound around her own dark locks, then she wound one around Venetia's chignon. They were laughing when a vibration in the air made Venetia turn around.

Ramón stood a few feet away watching them.

"What a charming scene," he commented. His deep brown tones struck a chord in her heart as he strode forward in a lightweight cream suit of immaculate cut. "I do not know which is the most charming, the tawny hair wreathed in flowers or the black."

He bent over Isabel, who held up the crystal ball and the doll, and took them in his brown fingers.

"So, you have two presents, little one. Very pretty."

He returned them to the small eager hands and gave his attention to Venetia. "You have had tea, Miss Mellor?"

Venetia nodded and found she had a difficulty in breathing beneath the enigmatic scrutiny of the dark eyes.

"Yes, thanks," she answered politely.

"Shall I order more tea, Señor Conde?" Luisa had risen rather agitatedly from her chair and in doing so sent the ball of wool from her knitting to spin at his feet.

He bent and scooped it up, returning it to the chair where her knitting lay.

"I have already had tea, Luisa. I came to tell you that Isabel will not be dining with us this evening. I have guests whom I do not wish she should meet. She will remain here with you." He smiled in friendly fashion at Luisa. It made a difference to his dark sardonic face, but, Venetia thought, it made his eyes look sad – disillusioned black eyes that were exciting, alluring and made one's heart beat with slow, thick strokes.

"You are ready to leave, Miss Mellor?" he asked politely.

They had gone through the cloistered walk and were turning

towards the Quinta when he stopped.

"Allow me," he said, and coolly began to unwind the chain of flowers from her hair.

There was a drift of after-shave lotion as he gently removed the clinging crown. His nearness made her nervous and she gave a small embarrassed laugh.

"I'd forgotten about the flowers," she gasped. "Isabel is rather sweet. I suppose she wanted to give me something back for the present."

She was hardly aware of what she was saying, for he had stopped unwinding the flowers and was looking down at the necklace around her slim throat. His fingers were cool against her warm throat as he lifted it slightly and she quivered.

"Fadrigo's handiwork, without a doubt. I trust you did not pay a lot for it," he commented dryly. "His work is quite expensive and he is a born salesman."

"I had it quite cheaply. In fact I was rather surprised when he priced it so moderately," she replied.

"Indeed?" The black brows lifted sardonically and he dropped the flowers into her hand. "You certainly made a considerable impression for him to let you off so lightly."

Venetia smiled impishly. "I did. He congratulated me upon my Spanish accent which I owe to you."

He turned and began to walk on and she followed suit, glancing up at the enigmatic profile.

"Fadrigo," he remarked with emphasis, "is quite a Don Juan with the ladies. He has ten children and is a much married man. He is not yet thirty. Also he is very partial to English women."

Venetia chuckled. "I noticed that. He said he would learn more English if it did not take so long."

"The lazy man's excuse."

Venetia laughed. "Maybe, as he said, he hasn't the time."

He looked down at her and his mouth quirked as the sudden gleam in his eyes collided with the little imps dancing in her own. So he was not without a sense of humour.

"Has he asked you to give him lessons?" he demanded, his eyes narrowing.

"Goodness, no!"

"Would you consider it if he asked?"

"I never gave it a thought." Her clear eyes widened. "Do you think he will?"

"Quite possibly. You will be wise to refuse if he does. His wife is a very jealous woman. In Spain the emotions, like the temperature, run high." He smiled down at her, a thin-lipped cruel smile. "Because a man has learned the art of self-control, women are apt to take it at face value, but beneath his conventional garb a man may still be wearing the red kerchief and the earrings. Never forget that, Miss Mellor, especially when you are abroad."

They had reached archways of the Quinta leading into the courtyard, where Ramón stopped and leaned against the portal to look down on her thoughtfully.

"You will go to visit my *novia* again, will you not?" he said evenly.

Venetia fingered the chain of flowers in her hands with her head down bent.

"Yes, unless you wish me not to," she replied.

"On the contrary, I would appreciate it if you would visit her whenever you can. I spend as much time with her as I can spare away from the business of running the estate. Two of my relatives are dining with us this evening at the Quinta – an uncle and aunt of mine – who are firmly in favour of putting my *novia* in a place for sick people."

Venetia had not lifted her eyes. She became engrossed in the flowers.

She said carefully, "I can see their point. They probably think it better for Señorita Valrosa to be with cases similar to her own."

He pushed his hands into the pockets of his trousers and digested this.

Then he said slowly, heavily, "What is your opinion?"

The question took her so much by surprise that she stared up at him speechless. She was startled by a strange new quality in his voice, one which she had not heard before. He was deeply concerned about Isabel and, while the knowledge brought a searing pain to her heart, she loved him all the more for it.

"Do you agree with my relatives that Señorita Valrosa will be better among those who are like her?" he insisted.

Her love for him filled her with a sudden warmth. He was asking her opinion of the most important thing in his life. His dark, saturnine features were washed away in a mist of tears. In its place she was seeing Isabel's enchanting small figure, the large, luminous, vacant eyes, the restless, small hands. Venetia blinked away the tears and spoke with the firm conviction of her heart.

"No, I don't agree with your relatives at all. In putting Señorita Valrosa away you'll be locking yourself away from the world too. Her condition is not congenital, which would be a different matter. She is as she is because of the accident and shock of losing her mother. There's no reason why she shouldn't recover her faculties some day. Has she no friends of her own age who would come to visit her to talk about old times and their own lives?"

"There have been friends calling from time to time, but they have ceased to call because they received no response from the poor child."

"Never mind." Venetia, with great effort, pushed the question and tensions filling her mind right away and gave a bright smile. "I'll go to see her wherever I can. We must hope for the best."

She held out her head to touch his sleeve and he took it between strong fingers.

"Thank you," he said, and raised her hand to his lips. "You have helped me more than you know. It has been a pleasure to talk to you and I thank you for it. I shall have the pleasure of your company at dinner this evening."

In her room, Venetia raised the hand Ramón had kissed to her cheek. It still burned from the impact of his cool lips. The courteous gesture had made her see that he would never regard her as anything more than a friend. Her only consolation was that she had been with him in his hour of need.

It suddenly occurred to her that she had not told him about Federico sending the crystal ball to Isabel. He would naturally think that she had bought both gifts herself. What did it matter? It was not important.

CHAPTER FIVE

IT was ten-thirty that evening before dinner was over. At half past eight, Venetia had descended the stairs to see Don Jorge crossing the hall and they had entered the dining room together. Ramón was there handing out drinks to his other guests, an elderly couple and a strikingly handsome young Spanish woman around the same age as herself.

Venetia was glad of Don Jorge's support, for three pairs of dark eyes alighting on her for the first time was rather intimidating.

"Ah," exclaimed Ramón, "may I introduce Tio Jorge's secretary, Miss Mellor. Miss Mellor, my Tio Carlos and Tia Alicia and Señorita Chimone Briño de Cortelez."

Venetia returned the gracious greeting of the elderly couple and the haughty young woman staring at her so curiously with a slight frown, warmly.

"Don Jorge." Chimone's rather hard tones caught everyone's immediate attention as she attached herself to him. "Ramon tells me you are writing a book. How terribly exciting! And how very clever of you."

She smiled up at him provocatively, drawing him down into the seat on the tapestry-upholstered sofa beside her.

Don Jorge smiled down into the charming face. "You will be wise to reserve judgement until you have read the book," he teased.

"All the same, it is an accomplishment and one that takes a certain amount of hard work. "I am very glad I do not have to work. I do not think I have the brains for it. But then men do not favour clever women, do they, Ramón?"

She flickered long lashes up at her host, who was handing her a glass of wine.

"It is enough, my dear Chimone, to have you around looking decorative and alluring," he said suavely.

Venetia, watching the girl's smug look of satisfaction, agreed with her first impression that Chimone was more striking than beautiful. Her mouth, small and beautifully modelled, was her best feature, along with her flawless peachy complexion. Her nose had a faint curve with slightly flaring nostrils and her eyes were set a little too close together for real beauty.

The aunt and uncle did not appear to be so formidable at second glance. Tia Alicia bore a faint resemblance to some of the family portraits on the walls of the Quinta. Straight-backed, they were conventionally attired in evening dress, Tio Carlos in a black suit and Tia Alicia in russet silk trimmed with fine old lace.

Later, seated at the dining table, they looked matriarchal, Venetia thought, as though they resented her intrusion into the family circle. Chimone was evidently a friend whom they had brought with them in order to tempt Ramón to break the chains that bound him to the unfortunate Isabel.

Conversation was, at first, desultory, but Ramón, the perfect host, was not long in putting Venetia at her ease. He encouraged Don Jorge's amusing flow of anecdotes with a gleam in his eyes which she found endearing and exciting. Utterly charming, he glowed with that inner male vitality of a disturbing personality. On the rare occasions that she met his dark eyes her heart was gripped by a powerful emotion utterly alien to her, as alien as the strange dark faces around her. He was very charming to Chimone, who hung on to his every word and made no secret of his admiration for him, a fact which, Venetia was sure, did not escape the hooded gaze of the aunt and uncle.

Venetia, tasting the innumerable courses and sipping the wine, was seeing another face in that richly furnished room, the face of Isabel. She was on Isabel's side as she watched the antics of the choice Spanish morsel the aunt and uncle were dangling before the eyes of their nephew.

After dinner, the ladies were served coffee on the heated loggia while the men enjoyed their cheroots. Chimone had planted herself in between Tia Alicia and Venetia.

"How long do you plan to stay in Spain, Miss Mellor?" she

asked, placing the cushions at her back to her liking.

Venetia turned to meet the cold glitter of a polite smile. Beneath the light of overhead lamps, Chimone's dark, vivid face was wholly Spanish.

"Until my services with Don Jorge are no longer needed," she answered quietly.

Chimone took her time at taking in the slim figure, the auburn hair, a halo beneath the light, the enchanting curve of the delicately moulded cheek and chin, and her black silky eyebrows drew together in a frown.

"Surely that could take some time. Will you not be homesick for your home, your friends?" A perceptible pause. "Your *novio*?"

Venetia smiled forbearingly. "I'm sure my stay will be far too pleasant for me to want to leave prematurely. Don Jorge is a delightful person to work for. Indeed, I shall be sorry to go when the time comes."

"You English are quite remarkable. Many of you have come to reside in this country without a qualm. For myself, I love my country and the way of life here. When I go on holiday, or a cruise, I enjoy it all the more because I know I shall be returning home at the end of it."

Venetia said crisply, "I love my country too, but I'm not maudlin about it. I go wherever my work happens to be."

"There is the difference, would you not agree?" Chimone's tone was condescendingly sweet. "I would find work a terrible bore. To do the same routine day after day, to be at someone else's beck and call. How terrible for you!"

"Not at all," Venetia assured her. "I'm afraid I would be bored if I had no work to do. My leisure is all the more enjoyable because of it, *señorita*."

"Really?" Chimone spoke in a bewildered manner which did not ring true. "I am not surprised to hear you talk thus, Miss Mellor. It would not surprise me to hear that your *novio* would consent to your working after marriage too. Such a thing would never be tolerated by a Spanish husband."

Coffee was served at that moment, and Venetia was prepared to drop the subject, realizing that, for some reason, Chimone was anxious to discover if she had a *novio*. The woman was too persistent for words. She must be very interested in Ramón, to be so interested in his uncle's secretary.

As for his aunt Alicia, she was hanging on to every word. Venetia sipped her coffee, found it delicious and relaxed. After all, what was she here for? She was being well paid and comfortably, indeed luxuriously, housed in exchange for her services to Don Jorge. The guests were another matter. They could treat her as they wished, air their views with the cool and calculated insolence of Chimone, who was attempting to belittle her in Doña Alicia's eyes she was sure of that. However, there was nothing to prevent her replying in the same vein to Chimone's rather impertinent remarks.

"As I have no *novio* I cannot enlighten you," she said coolly. "Have you a *novio, señorita*?"

"I have many admirers and was once affianced, but his family lost all their money, and we parted by mutual consent." Chimone spoke without emotion.

Venetia turned her eyes towards the long elegant throat as Chimone let her coffee slide down it.

"I'm sorry. You would be terribly upset," she said.

It was Doña Alicia's turn to speak. "There was no question of Chimone marrying a poor man who could not support her in the way to which she is accustomed. Tell me, Miss Mellor, this work you do for Don Jorge, is it a whim, curiosity to see the country, perhaps?"

"I work to live, Doña Alicia. It's as simple as that. I have a small annuity, but it's not sufficient to live on independently."

"You could marry a rich man, Miss Mellor," Chimone suggested coyly. "You are a pretty woman with feminine ways and you dress well. But I would advise you against taking a Spaniard for a husband. Our menfolk are very scornful about your Women's Lib we hear so much about. We women are all on the men's side of course."

Venetia was beginning to be fed up with her two companions and she said forcefully, "In a few years you will have no alternative other than to accept the changes progress will inevitably

75

bring into your lives. Incidentally, Women's Lib doesn't mean that the women want to rule the home. Far from it. The idea of the whole thing is that they should not be treated as chattels, unpaid housekeepers, by their husbands and to receive the same payment for any career they choose on equal merit."

The dead silence following this pronouncement was broken by the appearance of Don Jorge.

"Your presence, Doña Alicia and Señorita Cortalez, is requested by Ramón in the library," he informed the two women, who exchanged enigmatic glances as they rose to their feet.

"Mind if I smoke?"

Don Jorge's hand hovered near to the cheroot in his breast pocket. He had taken the chair beside Venetia and looked at her hopefully.

"Go right ahead," she said lightly. "I don't mind in the least."

The next few moments went by in silence as the pleasing aroma of the cheroot mingled with the night scents from the grounds of the Quinta. Stars twinkled in the dark blue sky and the shadows became more pronounced, the soft glow of the brazier and overhead lamps more golden.

"So you went to tea with Señorita Isabel this afternoon." Don Jorge drew blissfully on his cheroot and stared out over the garden.

Venetia was equally relaxed. It was easy to talk to Don Jorge. He was such a poppet. Now was the time to tell him about taking her sister's place.

He would understand. But would he trust her again? She could not bear that. Later, when he knew her better, she would tell him, but not now. So the moment passed.

"Such a tragedy," he went on as though to himself. "I sometimes wonder if she will ever recover."

"She is young," Venetia said warily.

Don Jorge sighed heavily. "Like Ramón, she does not grow younger."

"A most unenviable position for your nephew to be in," Venetia murmured inadequately.

76

"Indeed yes." Don Jorge sighed. "There are so many young women of wealth and good breeding who would only be too glad to be his wife. Not only is he good-looking and charming, he is a man of integrity. Once he has given his heart to a woman it will be for all time." He sighed again. "A great pity, since he will not marry unless his *novia* recovers."

Venetia swallowed on a lump in her throat. Don Jorge felt deeply on the matter of Isabel. She stared out into the night knowing that she felt something deeply too. Was it worth all this involvement to stay? she wondered.

Don Jorge continued, "It is a relief to talk to you, Miss Mellor, for I know you will treat everything I say as confidential. Just now Doña Alicia went to join my nephew and her husband in the library. They are very much against Ramón remaining a bachelor for so long. They brought the Señorita with them because they see her as a suitable match. My nephew met her at the winter sports in Switzerland two years ago. Like him, she is a good sportswoman, she can ski and knows how to handle boats. Furthermore, she is not after my nephew for his wealth and position. She is a wealthy young woman."

Venetia studied her hands in her lap. "Would you mind if your nephew married the Señorita Cortalez?"

"She would make him a dutiful wife. If he does decide to marry her it will have to be on his terms, for he will always make himself responsible for that poor unfortunate child."

Venetia could think of nothing to say. She longed to ask about Ramón's flat in London and whether he was thinking of returning there in the near future. But she knew her place. As an employee she had no right to discuss family matters. Don Jorge had obviously been upset by something which had occurred when the men had been left together after dinner. Otherwise he would not have confided in her. Later, Venetia went to her room knowing nothing of Ramón's future plans, and was made more uneasy by the fact that Don Jorge was still not aware of her true identity.

For the next few days Venetia worked hard with Don Jorge until

77

lunch time. The weather grew warmer and she began to spend her leisure time on the beach. Ramón and his *novia* had gone away, and after three days with no news of them, Venetia settled into a state of deep depression. That he should be away for so long with no whisper around of when he was returning was something she had to become accustomed to.

I'm no better than Carolyn drooling over the man, she told herself furiously. The only difference is that with Carolyn the feeling would not eat like acid inside her. Carolyn would not lose any sleep over any man.

It was small consolation to imagine them both in London where Carolyn would meet them and see the futility of her own plans regarding Ramón.

Don Jorge's health improved in the sea air and he was taking a dip in the sea before breakfast each morning. He had not commented on his nephew's absence from the Quinta. He was immersed in his book and Venetia wondered how long he planned to stay at the Quinta. She dithered alternately between longing for the more restful atmosphere of Don Jorge's home and the fear of their returning before Ramón came back.

Her plans for exploring the countryside were shelved as she clung to the Quinta in case he returned. The beach was the farthest she strayed, where there was no one but herself to enjoy the white stretch of sand and the blissful privacy. After her bathe she would stretch herself out to dry in the sun, her limbs spread-eagled as the warmth crept into her muscles already relaxed by her swim. Five minutes was enough in the heat before she was in the water again.

On the fourth day of Ramón's absence, Venetia was on the beach. Drying out after her bathe, she closed her eyes, her thoughts going back to her own mad dash to Spain and regretting now her mad reaction to a passing mood. Why had she allowed herself to be influenced by unknown forces within urging her on? It had been a mistake. She could see that now. The Spanish grandee and his poor *novia* had no place in the lives of the Mellor sisters.

It was possible that the re-entry of Chimone into his life had persuaded him to renew his efforts to find a cure for Isabel. He could have taken her to Madrid to consult the doctors there before going to London, and Carolyn.

There had been no word from her sister. Was it possible that she was finding her new job all-absorbing? Venetia sighed, wishing Carolyn would settle for Julian. They were ideally suited and Julian loved her to distraction. Pity he was not more prosperous. He would be in time, but Carolyn would not wait. Her interest in Ramón Aldenez had been increased by the fact that he had come into a title and a rich inheritance. With the Spanish grandee Carolyn would have everything for which she craved, wealth, position and the open sesame to all doors leading into the highest circles. Poor Carolyn! It was all so poignantly sad. Venetia's eyes closed to the steady lap of the waves against the shore.

When she opened her eyes again she was floating in a sea of fire. Drums throbbed in her temples and the swimsuit cut into her red swollen limbs. Struggling weakly, she pushed herself up in the hot sand. Of all the idiots, to have gone to sleep in the hot sun! The hand she put to her aching head was shaking as a feeling of nausea swept over her. The inside of her eyelids was blood red each time she blinked and the towelling robe she struggled into made her wince as it touched her scorched skin.

Venetia never did remember going back to the Quinta. She reached the blessed cool sanctuary of her room without meeting anyone and sank down on to the bed as blackness engulfed her. The attack of sunstroke was a severe one. For three days Venetia floated through a mist of pain during which a shadowy, white-clad figure gently oiled her sore body and applied cold compresses to her aching head.

The fourth day found her free from pain. The doctor had been and the kind, elderly nurse had brought her a noursihing soup when Don Jorge came.

"How are you, my child?" he asked, looking down at her with a smile.

"Much better, Don Jorge, thanks." Venetia pushed herself up into a sitting position in the bed and he placed the pillows more comfortably behind her back. "I'm awfully sorry," she rushed on. "We were going on so well with your book, and now I've not only brought you trouble but I'm also responsible for delaying its progress."

He patted her hand. "You are not to distress yourself. It is as much my fault as yours for not warning you about the danger of too much sun. However, apart from the pain you have suffered, no harm has been done. You must now eat well and soon we shall be able to resume our work on the book, which is of secondary importance to your health."

Venetia shook her head. "It's very kind of you, Don Jorge, to be so nice about it, but it doesn't alter the fact that I was very stupid to go to sleep in the sun."

Don Jorge said slowly, "When the mind is troubled we do silly things unconsciously. Our thoughts are divided instead of taking a steady course. Life is not easy for young people for they had so much to learn by experience. You have been happy in your work with me?"

Venetia lifted clear eyes to the kind dark ones. "I've loved it. Why do you ask? You have been satisfied with my work?"

"Absolutely satisfied, my child."

She laughed with relief. "Do you know, I feel really well today. How soon can we start work again?"

"We shall see."

Something in his tone struck a chill to her heart. He was acting very strangely. The last few words had been left hanging on the air – air which was becoming fraught with a menacing uncertainty. She waited.

"I have a surprise for you," he said.

"For me?"

Her voice was husky with the control she was putting upon herself.

"Your sister is here at the Quinta."

Venetia sank back into her pillows, thankful for their support. "You sent for her?" she gasped.

"No. She arrived last evening rather late, accompanied by

my nephew. Apparently they met in London and she came back with him."

Beads of moisture gathered on Venetia's brow. She had only one defence if Carolyn had already told him about them changing places, to behave as if nothing had happened and wait until he asked her about it. To confess now to her deception, a confession under duress, was unthinkable. She was no coward, and she would admit to her deception in Don Jorge's own good time.

He said kindly, "You have gone very pale, my child. Are you feeling all right?"

Venetia managed a smile. "Perfectly, thanks. It was rather a shock to hear of my sister's arrival, since she never wrote to tell me of her intention to visit me."

Feverishly, she wished he would go. He was so kind and she felt worse than if he had scolded her. She wanted to be alone, to prepare herself for her meeting with Carolyn, to know why she had come. A thought occurred and she looked up at him to say, "Does she know about my illness?"

He shook his head. "No. It was very late when they arrived and both my nephew and your sister retired to their rooms." Again he patted her hand. "Now do not worry. Just concentrate upon getting well."

She sat motionless for a long time after he had gone, her unseeing gaze fixed upon the door as it had closed behind him. Her thoughts ran around in her head like a demented hornet. How had Carolyn reacted when she had discovered that Ramón had been in Spain and that she, Venetia, had not let her know? She was seeing her sister again on the night she had burst into their flat in London to tell her the news of the Spanish grandee taking a flat nearby.

Her green eyes had glittered with excitement. "He's a Conde now – a real man – handsome, rich and terribly exciting, with a castle in Spain!"

It had awakened some strange kind of feeling in her, even then when her recollection of the Spanish grandee had been so dim, to hear Carolyn threaten to teach him a lesson for treating her so casually at Tamor Hall.

Venetia clenched her hands. Carolyn would not hurt him if she could prevent it, so strong was her love for him now. It was as deep and as unshakeable as the rugged mountain ranges forming an integral part of his beloved country.

Determinedly, Venetia left her bed and took a shower which did much to restore her feeling of weakness. Then she took a turn around the room, knowing that the nourishment she had received during her illness had kept up her strength and that the slackness she felt would soon wear off.

She forced herself to eat all her food when nurse brought it at lunch time, the last meal she was to bring now that Venetia was better. After a short siesta during which Venetia tried in vain to sleep, she washed and dressed.

A last peep in her mirror as she lightly made up her face assured her that she did not look at all bad. The brightness lacking in her hair would soon return. It was the brightness of her spirit that seemed dimmed for ever. She was taking a clean handkerchief from a drawer when the tap came on her door and her heart turned over as she gave permission to enter.

"So, you are up. Should you be?"

Ramón was striding across the room and Venetia, bereft of speech, felt the tension rising inside her. She was aware of everything about him at once, his dark face, the black eyes that could be hard or tender and, above all, his abundant energy. He stood above her again, having lost none of the exciting flavour of his personality. He had entered the room with the spontaneous gesture of a host concerned over a sick guest. Now she was again aware of his usual cool withdrawal from too close a contact.

"I'm quite recovered, thanks," she said.

Eagle-eyed and very dear, he stared down at her paleness, at the tawny hair cascading down on her shoulders and the vulnerable beat of a pulse at her temples.

His tone was less personal, yet strangely gentle. "Do not take it to heart. These things happen. You have yet to become acclimatised. It is sufficient to know that you are almost recovered. I say almost because I am wondering if you will feel up to

taking a short stroll in the grounds and calling on my *novia*."
He gave a half-smile and added casually, "You know, of course,
that your sister Carolyn is here in the Quinta? We arrived late
last evening, so I presume she will still be sleeping."

"Don Jorge told me this morning."

Venetia dropped her eyes, aware of the odd strained look in
his. He seemed to withdraw even more as he walked to the shut-
tered window to turn round and face her.

Haltingly, she told him, "I was going to take a stroll down to
the beach. I long to be out in the fresh air after such a long spell
in bed. I would be happy to go with you to see Señorita Valrosa.
I trust she is well."

"As well as can be expected," was the cool answer, and Venetia
knew by his tone that Isabel was no different.

He waited while she put on her sunglasses and a shady hat.
Her fingers shook as she pulled it on, knowing that she would
gladly suffer a hundred attacks of sunstroke, painful though
they were, to convalesce in his company.

He nodded approval at the hat. "I am pleased to see that you
are taking precautions. Sunstroke can be extremely painful. I
will take your arm in case you feel shaky."

At the feel of his fingers holding her firmly, Venetia knew it
was futile to fight the emotions his touch roused in her. She
simply had to accustom herself to his nearness, to the strength
of his body moving so effortlessly beside her. Outdoors the
grounds were bathed in a golden haze which intensified the
clarity of light. Was it foolish fancy or did the grounds really
take on a more poignant beauty? Strange how his presence
intensified her own delight in everything around her. Her
susceptibility to the beauties of nature filled her with a longing
to exclaim about them in her delight, but she held her tongue.
To admire the beauty he had lived with all his life would, no
doubt, be put down as a desire on her part to please.

He had slowed down his long stride to accommodate her
small one. Carolyn, Don Jorge, were forgotten. These golden
moments were hers, precious moments stolen from time which
would never occur again. They met no one in the grounds

apart from a few gardeners who were too far away to notice them.

"How are you feeling?" he asked.

They were passing white marble seats set beneath the shade of lemon trees.

"Fine, thanks," she answered, wondering if the weakness in her knees was due more to his nearness than to her stay in bed.

"We will rest for a while on one of these seats in the shade. I am convinced that you are still not a hundred per cent fit. You float along beside me like a piece of thistledown."

He led her to the shade of the trees away from sight of the Quinta. Venetia hugged one corner, giving him most of the seat in which to lower his long length. He hitched up his immaculate trousers and sat down.

"I am quite fit. I have always been slim. My weight is usually static. I don't have to slim," she vouchsafed.

"You are not feeling homesick?"

Venetia shook her head aware, of his arm along the back of the seat not far from her shoulder.

Defensively she answered, "No, I'm not. How was London?"

"There, you see, you have admitted it! You do miss the bright lights and your dates with all the young men."

Her clear eyes met his mocking ones steadily. "You're wrong. As a working woman I much prefer working conditions here to those in a crowded city."

"Was that your real reason for coming to Spain?"

"Why, of course. What other reason could there be?"

His voice was dry. "Quite a few."

"Then they're definitely not mine. I came in search of the sun. It was a rather peculiar feeling that I had to come – almost as if a voice was calling me."

She laughed, a small infectious laugh at her own absurdity.

"If the sun meant so much to you why did you not join Julian and Simon in Canada? California is not far away from there. Or even Australia?"

Her tawny eyes were clear of guile as she looked at him. "For one thing, there was a job waiting here which spelt safety." Again the small laugh, this time a little self-consciously. "I'm afraid I'm not one of those Amazon women who can set out to conquer worlds and are all self-sufficient. I must confess to being wholly feminine. I'm a coward at heart and tremble at the first step into the unknown."

He said on a note of satire, "For a timid person you are doing very well. I would say that the adventurous spirit burning inside you was anything but weak. I have the same opinion of your sister Carolyn. Indeed, I was surprised to discover that she had not been married at least twice. She was decidedly coquettish and very enchanting even at sixteen."

His tone jarred a little on her sensitive ear. He sounded cynical and wholly disapproving. What had got into him? Venetia tried to think what she had said wrong and found nothing. It would have been easy to tell him why Carolyn had not married, easy to say Carolyn would have been married years ago had Julian been a wealthy man.

But Carolyn's life was her own to do with as she liked. Venetia stole a glance at her beloved Spanish grandee sitting so elegantly beside her. What did he know of wanting a thing so desperately that everything else faded into insignificance beside it? Not that she agreed with Carolyn's slant on life, far from it. Venetia studied the dark profile, her mind a welter of conflicting emotions. He was staring ahead to the lemon trees screening the villa of his *novia*. The fine bone structure of the well shaped head the wide shoulders, the fastidious poise of his lean frame as he relaxed in his seat indicated wealth, breeding and an experience of a world that had always been his oyster.

Of what or whom was he thinking? Isabel or Carolyn? Had her sister made an impression on him after all? Did he look back longingly to those days at Tamor Hall? Venetia wished she knew.

The red car flashed by in the sun behind the lemon trees. She sat up in pleasurable surprise as she recognised it.

"Isn't that Don Jorge's grandson? He's calling at the villa," she exclaimed. "How nice!"

Pleasure had warmed her voice and Ramón turned his head

slowly to look at her glowing face. Venetia thought with sudden inconsequence how incredibly dark his eyes were and lowered her own in confusion.

"You like Federico?" he asked evenly.

"Yes, very much." She touched her lips with the tips of her fingers. "I've just remembered something," she said. "He bought your *novia* the crystal ball." Venetia laughed. "I bought the flamenco doll."

He smiled. "Federico has brought some manuscripts of Don Jorge's and is calling to take tea at the villa on his way." He rose to his feet. "Shall we go and join them?"

The short walk to the villa was one of enchantment with the sunlit scene created just for them. The fountain sent rainbow sprays in the scented air and flowers were everywhere. Federico was rummaging in the boot of his car when they reached him outside the villa. He had a parcel in his hand and upon seeing Venetia reached for another gaily wrapped one from the boot. This he handed to her with a white smile.

"*Buenos dias*, Miss Mellor," he said. "Mother sends you her regards with this small present and hopes, as I do, that you are fully recovered from your illness."

Venetia's eyes misted as she accepted the gift. "How sweet of Doña Matilde, and you too. I have fully recovered. I hope Doña Matilde is well?"

"*Muy bien, gracias.*" Federico gave a little bow. "It is good to see you again. We have missed you."

Venetia laughed. "Surely I haven't been long enough with you to be missed? It's very nice of you to say so, all the same."

He waved an expressive hand. "It is true, I assure you. We Spaniards take the sun for granted. It is there, but we see it not. But when a sunbeam enters our household, then leaves, we are sad."

"Thanks, no one has ever likened me to a sunbeam before. Do thank Doña Matilde for me." Venetia kissed Federico's cheek, and suddenly Ramón's fingers were curling cruelly around her arm.

"Be warned, Miss Mellor. Our friend here is adept at making

flowery speeches. You will soon hear him paying similar ones to my *novia*," he said forcefully. "Shall we go in?"

Within the cool interior of the villa they sat down to tea with Isabel admiring the present Federico had bought. She had the coloured crystal ball in her hands when they had entered the room and she had relinquished it for the parcel Federico gave to her. Doña Matilde had sent a musical box and Isabel's small white hands caressed it delightedly. Venetia had not unwrapped Doña Matilde's gift. She had decided to leave opening it until she returned to the Quinta.

For her, that afternoon was yet another incident which she could hug jealously to her heart for ever – her beloved Spanish grandee sitting next to her, his eyes very dark beneath silky brows, his teak skin touched with shadows around the high cheekbones and temples – Federico, laughing, young and handsome, scattering compliments indiscriminately to Isabel and herself.

Isabel sparkled too, with a flower in her dark hair and her lovely mouth sweetly curved with delight as she passed the box to Federico to wind it up again and again during tea. The tune was wholly Spanish and one could imagine the castanets clicking gaily. Years afterwards Venetia recalled that day as having a dreamlike quality about it for her. Everyone seemed completely happy. Even Luisa's black dress rustled approval as she waited upon them, her dark face beaming.

The small packet beside Venetia's plate was, so Ramón said, from Isabel. It was a pair of ear-rings with a matching dress clip of diamonds cascading from the pin. A hint of mockery danced in Ramón's eyes at her heightened colour.

"It's beautiful, but much too expensive," she exclaimed.

"My *novia* chose it herself," he assured her, his mockery changing to satire as he added, "She obviously shares the opinion of the more enlightened women of other countries that diamonds are a girl's best friend."

"You're teasing." Venetia whispered, aware of Isabel and Federico being too engrossed in the rewinding of the music box to notice them. "I am sure your *novia* would have no idea

87

of its value and would choose it for its glitter. It's far too expensive for me to accept and you know it."

She was quite unprepared for the long fingers closing over her own as they curled around the jewel box.

"It is enough that my *novia* wished you to have it and would be upset if you refuse to accept it. You will please do so."

The close grip of his hand was like a fire consuming her whole being. When he released it her hand was shaking so much she had to place it on the table, presently slipping the gift into her handbag.

"Thanks," she managed at last as the music from the box began to tinkle again. "I wish I could give her the one gift she needs so much – that of restoring her to health."

"That is very sweet of you." His tones sounded extra deep and she missed the sudden gleam, no more than a flash, in the dark eyes as they rested upon her averted profile. "Unfortunately, we are not given the power to perform miracles."

Later, in her room at the Quinta, Venetia closed her door and leaned against it, recalling the incidents of the last few hours. She had been reluctant to leave the villa with the shutters drawn to keep out the heat and the fingers of light pushing between the slats to fall across the happy group seated at the table. Federico had driven Ramón and herself the short distance back to the Quinta in his car. She had sat between them in the front seat, only too aware of Ramón's closeness. Federico had left them in the hall to seek Don Jorge and they had walked to the foot of the stairs. With her foot on the first step, he had placed cool fingers against her flushed cheek.

"You are flushed," he said gravely. "Your head is free from pain? You are sure you are feeling all right?"

Small wonder that beneath his obvious concern Venetia had found herself smiling rather foolishly. The touch of his fingers, the dark eyes looking deeply into her own, were the final touches to an afternoon she would never forget.

"No pain," she assured him, only the pain in her heart.

Numbly, she looked down at the parcel from Doña Matilde in her hand. She opened it sitting down upon the bed and gazed at a beautiful Spanish shawl delicate as a cobweb with a deep golden fringe.

"It's gorgeous!" she exclaimed after recovering her breath, and hastened to the dressing table mirror to drape it around her shoulders. It really was the loveliest thing she had ever seen. The colours were exquisite as she twisted this way and that to see the effect. Over an evening dress the result would be breathtaking. So lost was she in the beauty of it that the knock on her door startled her profoundly.

Venetia swung round to see Carolyn enter and was reminded once again of her good looks, the rich titian hair, the green eyes, the practised poise of her lovely figure sophisticated to the point of being insolent as she closed the door and leaned against it menacingly. The angry rise of her well-defined bust beneath the silk wrap told only too plainly that she had a score to settle.

Venetia braced herself to meet it. "Hello, Carolyn. You might have let me know you were coming. How are you?"

Carolyn almost spat in her fury. "You have a nerve!" she began. "You expect me to let you know my movements when you've been so secretive about your own? Why should I let you know I was coming? Did you tell me about travelling here to Spain with the Spanish grandee? You thought it was a huge joke, didn't you, leaving me waiting for him in London when all the time he was with you!" Her breath rasped. "You've been very clever, but not clever enough. You have no idea how sorry you're going to be that you came!"

Venetia walked to the bed and sank down on it weakly. Pushing back the hair from her hot forehead, she stared bemusedly.

"What do you mean? I've done nothing wrong," she whispered.

"No, you haven't put a foot wrong since you so suavely suggested taking my place, have you? Why didn't you let me know you'd travelled here with Ramón?"

"I did in my last letter, which you evidently haven't received. I wrote almost a week ago – it must be in the post. I would have told you before, but I was expecting Ramón to return to the flat in London any time. I. . . ."

"You knew he wasn't returning to London. A likely story!" Carolyn cut in furiously. "A letter in the post, indeed! I'll believe that when I see it. You never intended to tell me anything. What a good time you've had, laughing up your sleeve, telling Don Jorge Moreno how happy you were to step into the place your sister had left so heartlessly vacant in order that he would not be inconvenienced. No doubt you told Ramón too, or do you call him the Spanish grandee?"

"We're not on first name terms. He refers to me as Miss Mellor."

Venetia had gone very pale and the green eyes narrowed, grew calculating.

"Really? I wonder why. We always addressed each other by our first names at Tamor Hall."

Carolyn strolled up to the bed. Her smile was gloating and she said softly, "There's only one explanation for that. You haven't told Señor Moreno that you've taken my place, have you? Is that why Ramón calls you Miss Mellor, because you've taken him into your confidence about the switch between us?"

Venetia's mouth tightened. "I refuse to say anything until you've cooled down. It's your fault I came over here in the first place. If you'd taken the job I wouldn't be here."

They looked at each other like enemies and Carolyn strolled to a chair which gave a view of herself in the dressing table mirror and sat down.

"You are not in a position to tell me to do anything," she stated, crossing long, slim legs and looking at her reflection in the mirror. "But do go on."

Venetia dropped the shawl from shoulders growing sticky in the heat. Her head was beginning to throb and Carolyn's attitude did not help.

She moistened dry lips. "How did you know I travelled here with Ramón? Did he tell you himself?"

"I bumped into Jean Ashe back from her honeymoon in Spain. She and her husband sat behind you on the plane and heard you talking to him. What did you tell him about me? I hope

90

you didn't say anything about Julian and me?"

"I told him all the news, but I also told him you were still unmarried and quite free. I don't think he knows anything about your affair with Julian, unless Julian has written to him. The Spanish grandee is no fool. He knew I'd taken your place directly I told him where I was bound for. You'd asked Don Jorge to refer to him as having made your acquaintance."

"Yes, I did. I'd forgotten. What I can't understand is why you didn't send me a card or something when you landed in Spain telling me of your meeting."

Venetia shrugged resignedly. "I told you, I was waiting to see what he was planning to do. For all I knew his trip home could have been a business one after which he would return to his flat in London."

"I don't believe you." Carolyn's eyes were hard as flint. "You were hoping he would stay in Spain. I wouldn't put it past you engineering the invitation to stay at the Quinta."

Venetia blushed and lowered her head. "Don't be silly," she said tightly. "Don Jorge has been ill and Ramón invited him to the Quinta for the sea air."

Carolyn cried accusingly, "What are you blushing for? Your guilty conscience, I suppose. I believe you went down with sunstroke. Did Ramón hold your hand?"

"Why are you being so beastly?" Venetia flashed indignant tawny eyes. "Why would he hold my hand when he was against Don Jorge taking you on as his secretary?"

Carolyn stared unbelievingly. "I don't believe it."

"It's true. He wanted Don Jorge to engage a young Spanish writer, a man who can speak several languages fluently."

"Then why was I selected for the post?" Carolyn demanded.

"Because he's writing the book for English publishers, I suppose, or just to show he was not going to be dictated to whom he should employ by Ramón Aldenez."

Carolyn smiled. "So Señor Moreno received you quite happily when you arrived, thinking you were me?"

Venetia nodded. "I haven't got round to telling him yet that I'm not the person he engaged."

"Too busy ingratiating yourself with Ramón, I suppose." Carolyn leaned forward in her chair. For some reason the sight of Venetia fingering the silken gold fringe of the Spanish shawl lying across her knee infuriated her. Her voice rose. "How far have you progressed with him, and what else have you been keeping from me?"

"Keep your voice down," Venetia whispered urgently. "The maids swarm along the corridors like flies. I will not have Don Jorge upset so soon after his illness. He's a very kind and nice man."

"What about upsetting me? I'm your sister and I could do with a bit of consideration too. What about Ramón's fiancée?"

"What about her? They're engaged and that's that. No doubt Ramón has told you about her."

Venetia began to wilt. She did not feel up to the kind of cross-examination Carolyn was handing out. Her tawny eyes looked troubled.

Carolyn waved a hand disparagingly. "I know he'd taken her to specialists on periodical visits. How long do you think he can remain faithful to a shell of a woman? He's much too virile and healthy to lead a celibate life indefinitely."

Venetia quivered. "You know an awful lot about a man whom you haven't met for six years until recently."

Carolyn's smile was a knowing one. "I learned to know him quite well at Tamor Hall. You were far too busy playing childish games with Simon. You still haven't grown up if you think you can get the better of me."

"No one wants to get the better of you. Really, Carolyn, what has got into you? What do you intend to do, spend a holiday here at the Quinta?"

Carolyn studied her nails and Venetia looked at her anxiously. "I might."

She spoke offhandedly, but Venetia was not deceived. There was certain to be some plan building up beneath that lovely titian hair.

"What about your new job? Are they happy about you taking a holiday so soon?" she asked.

"Oh, that!" Carolyn looked at her reflection in the dressing table mirror and touched up her hair with a well manicured hand. "I've given it up. I couldn't stand watching all the wealthy clients dressed to kill buying beauty aids which couldn't make them beautiful in a hundred years. The old bags!"

"You might be one of them yourself one day," Venetia retorted.

"Don't worry, no one is going to make me old before my time working my fingers to the bone to live. That's why I hope Julian is chatting up some millionaire's daughter in Canada. It will be one way out of his difficulties."

She raised a hand delicately to her mouth and stifled a yawn as if the subject bored her.

"Serve you right if he does marry someone else," Venetia said indignantly. "You would be green with envy if he did, especially if she was wealthy. You're a fool, Carolyn. You don't know when you're lucky."

But Carolyn was not listening. She was leaning forward to pick up a corner of the Spanish shawl.

She said enviously, "Where did you get this lovely thing? Did Ramón give it to you?"

"No. Doña Matilde, Don Jorge's daughter, sent it to me. She's a very sweet person and I like her very much."

"She must be very generous to give you this. It's beautiful. Is she married, then?"

"Doña Matilde is a widow with a son, Federico, in his twenties. Her husband died two years ago and they both came home to Don Jorge. Federico manages the estate. He called this morning with a manuscript for Don Jorge. He has a red car. Didn't you see him?"

"No." Carolyn dropped the shawl and, leaning back in her chair, linked her fingers behind her head. "He might come to the party Ramón is giving this evening. Tell me about his relations and friends. He has quite a few uncles and aunts, according to Rosa the maid – Ramón, I mean."

"Carolyn!" Venetia protested in a shocked whisper, looking up from her task of folding the Spanish shawl. "Surely you haven't been questioning the staff? What an awful thing to do.

93

Suppose Ramón found out? He would be furious. How could you?"

Her sister shrugged carelessly. "My dear girl, don't you know that the best way to find out anything about a family is to question the staff? As for Ramón finding out, I doubt if he ever comes within speaking distance of most of the maids." She drew a cigarette case from the pocket of her wrap and lighted a cigarette. "What about a certan Chimone something or other who came to dinner recently with relatives of Ramón's?"

"You mean Chimone Brino de Cortalez? Ramón's relatives are anxious for him to put his *novia* into a home and marry someone else. Chimone, apparently, is a hot favourite, being wealthy, very attractive and obedient."

Carolyn blew out a derisive line of smoke and admired her reflection in the mirror. "Obedient my foot," she scoffed. "Why, half the fun of being married to Ramón would be gone without an argument once in a while. Just think of the thrill of making it up again. I bet there'd be no half measures with him."

Venetia said darkly, "Don't underestimate him. He might beat you into submission."

Carolyn laughed. "Like to bet that he won't marry his Isabel?"

Venetia's mouth curved tenderly. "Poor Isabel. She really is sweet."

"She's an imbecile, isn't she? Nothing sweet about that."

"It was an accident that could easily happen to anyone."

Carolyn rose to her feet. "It didn't happen to Ramón, so why should he pay for it? Did you know he's giving the dinner party this evening in my honour? He's anxious to return the hospitality we gave to him during his visit to Tamor Hall. I have no idea of the number of guests, but don't monopolize him, will you? I want him all to myself. See you later!"

When Carolyn had gone, Venetia lay back on her bed and stared up at the ornate ceiling. What new set of problems her sister's visit to the Quinta would bring were, as yet, an unknown quantity. She only knew that Carolyn was out to get the Spanish grandee and would allow nothing to stand in her way. Wearily, she closed her eyes and slept.

By the time she dressed for dinner that evening, her headache had gone, banished by the sleep that afternoon after Carolyn had gone. Her dress, a pure silk chiffon, flower-designed, in eau de nil with long flowing sleeves and a demure neckline, was a perfect foil for the Spanish shawl. Both Carolyn and herself were fortunate to have a dressmaker who made and designed their clothes to suit their personality. The Mellor sisters, she said, made her task of making their clothes easy since they had a faultless eye for fashion and knew exactly what suited them. They knew that on a limited income they had to choose fashion pieces which could be swapped about and used over and over again.

As Venetia guessed, Carolyn's dress was eyecatching. She entered the room like a film star at a preview of her film, her eyes alighting on the Spanish shawl draped around Venetia's shoulders.

"Very nice," she commented without rancour.

"You look fabulous!" Venetia exclaimed, admiring the gossamer, shimmering silk dress with its snow white camisole top, long slinky sensuous skirt and hip jacket collared in white nylon fur.

"Like it?"

Her sister twirled around in an exaggerated poise, admiring herself in the dressing table mirror.

"It's beautiful." Venetia picked up her evening bag and watched the familiar pout on her sister's lips replace the look of smug satisfaction.

"I suppose it does help when you wear a dress with flair and imagination, but it still doesn't make it an exclusive model. Some day I'm going to have the real thing. Just you wait!"

Carolyn tossed her head defiantly and opened the door with a grand gesture.

"I hope you find it worth it," Venetia said, following her out of the room.

In the great hall below, beautifully dressed women and immaculately tailored men were arriving for dinner. Ramón, handsome in evening dress, was greeting his aunt Alicia and uncle Carlos. They were accompanied by Chimone, who was eyecatching with diamonds scintillating around her throat and in her ears. The jewelled comb in her jet black hair added to the glamour of red lips and flashing dark eyes as she smiled up coquettishly at her host.

"Who is the Spanish beauty ogling Ramón?" Carolyn whispered urgently as they drifted downstairs.

"That's Chimone Briño de Cortalez," Venetia replied, with an odd pain clutching her heart as his white smile flashed down at the dark, attractive face.

"Nuff said," Carolyn commented, taking in Chimone's model evening dress in ruby satin and lace. "Here we go to battle stations!"

Venetia did not reply. Chimone might be attractive, but Ramón could be more interested this evening in red hair, green eyes and a pale camellia skin. Then they were being greeted by Ramón. A moment or two of quivering awareness and Venetia moved on, leaving Carolyn to have an extra word with him.

No one could live in the Quinta Aldanez without being constantly aware of the luxuriousness of the place. Yet not until that moment did Venetia appreciate just how wealthy the Spanish grandee was. There was an aura of wealth in the aroma of expensive cigars, mature wine and good food rising tantalizingly to the nostrils and palate. To Venetia, it was intimidating to say the least. Carolyn, no doubt, could carry it off superbly, might even hook the man in the end. But Venetia did not flatter herself that he would ever be more than remotely interested in her except as Carolyn's sister.

In the dining room, the long table was decorated with candelabra. Crystal glass and silver sparkled among flower arrangements and servants were drawing out the tapestry-upholstered chairs to seat the guests. The rustle of expensive gowns soon subsided as everyone took their allotted place and Venetia found herself seated on one side of Ramón with Carolyn on the other.

There was utter silence when their host rose to his feet and, with great charm, welcomed publicly the presence of the Mellor sisters in their midst. He told his guests that he had spent some of the happiest moments of his life at Tamor Hall and assured them that English hospitality was second to none.

Dinner progressed through innumerable courses, each one excellently prepared and served in portions of the right amount enabling one to enjoy every course and yet not overeat. Don Jorge sat on Venetia's other side and Venetia turned his way often during the meal since Carolyn was demanding the whole of her host's attention.

Towards the end of the meal, Don Jorge was engaged in conversation with a rather austere man seated next to him, leaving Venetia to eat in silence.

"You are very quiet." Ramón's deep tones aroused her as he smiled down at her averted profile. "I trust you are not deploring the fact that I have not invited my *novia* here this evening. It would have been unkind to bring her to be the cynosure of all eyes. She would not have enjoyed it," he said gravely.

She said quickly, "Why should you conclude that my silence was merely meditation on behalf of Señorita Valrosa?"

"Because you are the kind of person who feels deeply for the less fortunate, too deeply, since there is nothing to be done in the case of my poor Isabel. You see, I am beginning to know you very well."

But not too well, her heart begged silently. She could bear almost anything, but not that he should discover her love for him. Her voice was low.

"You question my feelings, yet your own are equally deep for others, otherwise you would not remain true to your *novio*. Is that not so?"

"My compassion certainly is deep, but circumstances sometimes govern the way we live. Until now I was content to let things lie, but I am discovering that I am only human after all."

The misery on his face was a fleeting shadow which she glimpsed with a confused emotion as he turned to answer Carolyn, who had addressed him. Then she pulled herself together determinedly, for what he said was true, she did feel

97

other people's troubles far too much. Miserably she knew that it was not her nature to be different. It was as impossible as the quenching of her passion for him, this love that ate into her heart and made her a mindless fool. She had got to fight it. She must, since it was obviously her sister's influence that was gradually undermining his devotion to Isabel. It was Carolyn to whom he would turn in his bid for freedom from his intolerable burden.

"May I join you?"

The accented English was spoken in husky tones as Venetia and her sister were seating themselves on one of the ornate couches in a salon to which the ladies had retired leaving the men to their cigars and wine, after dinner.

Chimone was bearing down upon them with gushing friendliness.

"Please do," Carolyn murmured, winking surreptitiously at Venetia as she moved up in her seat in order to make room for the Spanish girl between them.

Then began for what seemed to Venetia to be the strangest part of a strange evening as Chimone and Carolyn played a game of words, leaving her to listen bemusedly. But clever as Chimone was at asking leading and often personal questions, Carolyn proved to be more than a match for her.

While Chimone had not actually regarded Don Jorge's secretary as being a potential rival, her lovely, redheaded, self-possessed sister had given her food for thought. This much occurred to Venetia as she listened, hating the subterfuge and shallow gesture of friendship from the inquisitive Chimone. The first day up from her bed had been a long one and she was relieved when they reached the end of a long and eventful evening with the guests taking their leave. Carolyn had gone off somewhere with Ramón when she made her way slowly up the staircase to her room. All the guests had gone, and fearful of what she would find if she were to go in search of her host to thank him for a pleasant evening, Venetia settled for going to bed.

"Miss Mellor, your presence is needed in the library."

Ramon's voice was like a pistol shot aimed at her head. Slowly she turned half way up the staircase to see him below striding towards her from the direction of the library. She lifted eyelids beginning to ache with tiredness and wondered what could be so important that it could not wait until the morning. His face was set. They were walking across the hall now and he was holding her elbow in the firm grip that made her quiver inside. At the entrance to the library he paused and the quiver inside her changed to a feeling of apprehension as, moving abruptly away from him, she entered the room.

Don Jorge and Carolyn were the only occupants. Carolyn was sitting near the huge desk-like table, lovely slim legs crossed, a drink in her hand. There was a hard light in her eyes which alerted Venetia to be on her guard as Don Jorge rose to his feet from a seat nearby. She was seated in silence, Ramón put a drink in her hand and moved to the fireplace to stand by Don Jorge, who was looking rather uncomfortable.

It was Carolyn who broke the uneasy silence. "Poor Venetia," she cooed. "You look worn out, poor pet, and no wonder, taking on a job you were thrust into in order to fill the breach until I could come to relieve you."

Before Venetia could gather her scattered wits, Carolyn continued,

"Never mind. You'll be able to have a long rest, for Don Jorge has very kindly invited you to his home for a holiday and to recuperate after your attack of sunstroke. Isn't it kind of him?" The smile did not reach the green eyes and her tone, honeysweet, was relentless to Venetia's painful vulnerability. "I've told Don Jorge you won't be able to stay long because of leaving our flat unattended." Her smile at the two men was graciousness itself. "You have no idea the amount of housebreaking that goes on in London. Have they, dear?"

Venetia gazed upon her sister's practised smile, numb and speechless with surprise and shock. Poor Don Jorge was looking at her with a puzzled frown in the fine dark eyes. As for Ramón, he was regarding her with the old unsmiling consideration with which he had greeted her that day on the plane.

Only Carolyn was unperturbed, indeed in spite of her loving sister act, Venetia knew she was enjoying herself. She smiled brightly at both men.

"I would like to thank you both for being so kind to my little sister," she told them evenly. "I was rather worried at sending her here alone, but it was impossible for me to come at the time stated to take up my new job. There were important matters for me to attend to before I could discharge myself honourably from my former post. But I'm sure you will understand."

Venetia, hearing her sister's voice droning on from far away, thought despairingly that half the truth was better than none. It would have been easy for her to tell her own side of the story. After all, it was her word against Carolyn's. But the damage had been done. Wrangling would not alter the fact that everything had been spoiled. Her face lost its colour and she gazed down into the wine in her glass with the knowledge that she would remember the scene before her to her dying day. She wanted desperately to escape from Carolyn's treachery, Don Jorge's concerned regard and most of all from Ramón's stony silence.

Slowly, shakenly, she put down her untouched drink on the low table near her elbow and rose to her feet. Mercifully, Don Jorge was the only one directly concerned in the little drama so ingeniously arranged by her sister, and it was to him she spoke.

Her face pale as alabaster, she began, "Don Jorge, I owe you an apology for not telling you that I'd taken my sister's place. I'm very sorry for causing you all this trouble, including the inconvenience of my being in bed with sunstroke. I hope you'll forgive me."

Her voice steadied as pride came to her aid. Her eyes, however, were misty and she hoped to keep them clear enough to make a dignified exit when she had said her piece. She did not feel the Spanish shawl slip from her shoulders on to the ground. She stood rigid, her hands gripping her evening bag in front of her, staring at him filled with an unbelievable shame.

"I . . . I don't want to sound ungracious and . . . I do appreciate your kind invitation for . . . for me to stay for a while. . . . What I'm trying to say is . . . well, I'm leaving first thing in the morning for home, with due regard to the Señor Conde, whom I wish to thank for his kind hospitality."

Venetia could not have looked at Ramón had her life depended upon it and she hung on to Don Jorge's gaze like a lifeline. He lifted startled brows, then said on a note of protest,

"But, my child, you have not recovered fully from your attack of sunstroke. You are not fit enough to make the journey yet. Let me persuade you to stay for at least a week. Doña Matilde would love to see you again – in fact she will never forgive me if I allow you to leave without saying goodbye to her. It would give me great pleasure to know that you were enjoying the benefit of a week with her. Do say you will stay."

Venetia shook her head. "I'm sorry, Don Jorge, I've delayed you in your work long enough. I'm sure you'll be pleased to see the back of me. Thank you again for all your kindness. And you, Señor Conde. Goodbye."

Blindly, she turned and made for the door, but someone else reached it before she did. The Spanish shawl was draped around her shoulders and the door opened. Venetia knew it was Ramón, but she dared not look up in case the tears flowed. She flitted across the hall like a ghost and ran up the stairs, not stopping until she reached her room.

She was lying on her bed staring unseeingly up at the ceiling when Carolyn walked in. The window shutters were open and moonlight filled the room.

Venetia did not move. She ignored Carolyn standing by her bed and did not even look at her.

Carolyn said, "I'm sorry it had to be this way, but you'll have to admit I was right. Everything has been settled with the minimum of fuss. I shall take over from you with Don Jorge and go on from there. The only thing I don't like is you going back home so soon. You could stay for a week or so. You say you like Doña Matilde and you won't be staying here at the Quinta where you would meet Don Jorge each day."

Venetia closed her eyes and was silent, and Carolyn made an

impatient gesture with an expressive movement of her hand.

"Why don't you say something?" she demanded. "You must see that I couldn't stay on indefinitely as Ramón's guest. Working for Don Jorge means that I can stay here for two years, time enough for me to convince Ramón that I'm the wife he needs."

She walked to the window to stare out into the night and for several moments the only sound in the room was Venetia's little travelling clock on the small bedside table. She had been listening to Carolyn trying to justify her treachery and tried to convince herself that it was not a dream. But Don Jorge's disappointment in her, Ramón's stony mask, had been real enough. Her hands clenched.

"Will you go now?" she said at last. "I shall have to be up early to pack in the morning. Oblige me by staying in your room until I've gone. I never want to see you again. If you want Ramón you'll have to fight every inch of the way to make him change his mind about his fiancée. But that won't be any problem for you, since you aren't too scrupulous about the methods you use. Now get out!"

Carolyn walked back to the bed. "I can't go until I tell you about that job with my late boss. I'm not entirely heartless. You'll find he'll be more than willing to give you a trial. He's tried several girls, but none of them have suited. You have only to write to him and I'll give you the gen."

She continued to do so until Venetia turned her back and covered her head with the bedclothes. At last her voice trailed away into silence. The door opened and closed. Carolyn had gone.

CHAPTER SIX

VENETIA awoke the following morning from a troubled night's sleep. As the events of the previous evening invaded her thoughts, she winced. There was none of the usual pleasurable anticipation at facing a new day, and the sun streaming in through her window did nothing to lighten her dark and dismal thoughts. Since her decision to leave, Venetia had made no plans. It would be a good idea to look around Barcelona until she could book a flight home, but beyond that she could not think.

Her packing had been completed when Rosa arrived with her breakfast tray. Her surprise on seeing the packed suitcases changed to consternation when she learned that Venetia was leaving soon after breakfast and would require a taxi from the nearest garage.

In shocked tones, she exclaimed, "No one leaves the Quinta in a taxi, Miss Mellor. There are always cars available for the guests. The Señor Conde sees to that. I will make enquiries."

Rosa returned to say that the car would be ready within the hour, and she stared in dismay at the untouched breakfast. Was it not to Venetia's liking? Did Miss Mellor not feel well? She looked a *pequeña palida*, *perdonar*. "Some coffee, freshly made, *tal vez*?"

But Venetia shook her head, gave Rosa a generous tip and thanked her for her services. The girl seemed genuinely sorry to see her leave and went away with great reluctance when Venetia said she would not be required. Venetia was ready well within the hour, having dressed with her usual care. If she was to leave the Quinta, she would do so with dignity, she told her reflection as she jammed the white straw hat on her tawny hair and looked with a kind of defiant appraisal at the smart cream check dress. She looked cool and crisp and in no way as dejected as she felt. Her colour rose as the last approaching minutes of her presence in the Quinta drew to a close. Putting her fingers up to a burning hot cheek, Venetia walked to the window to take a last look at the view she had begun to love.

Sadly, she gazed out on to the immaculate grounds, bland and smiling in the sun, and looked longingly at the white beach meandering down to a placid blue sea of polite ripples. Pity there had not been time for a last swim. It was better to be away as quickly as possible, to cut all ties ruthlessly and try to forget. In the world of business one could eventually manage to lose oneself, to tire the body and the brain by work until sleep claimed what was left. She might even apply for a job up North where new surroundings would numb the pain in her heart. Carolyn had not appeared when Manuel, one of Ramón's chauffeurs, came to collect her cases and she followed him downstairs.

Nor was she outside. She had evidently thought better of it. Venetia adjusted her sunglasses as they approached the car with the coat of arms on the door. Then, as the chauffeur went to put her cases in the boot, a tall figure appeared striding swiftly towards them. Manuel was dismissed in crisp Spanish after putting the cases in the boot and Ramón was opening the car door for Venetia. No word was spoken.

He slid into the driving seat beside her and handling the car with his usual skill, swung it around to drive away at speed. There was no time to catch a last painful glimpse of the Quinta. So ends my two years in the sun, Venetia thought bitterly, and looked down at her hands in her lap. But she was not seeing her hands. She could see only the Spanish grandee's dark, expressionless face as he sat beside her.

So she sat for a long time, her hands clasped with deceptive tranquillity and her thoughts confused as to why Ramón should take it upon himself to see her off the premises, as it were. He certainly could not do it quick enough, for the speed he checked up was terrific. And yet he was the one who was driving her on the first stage of her homeward journey. Venetia hugged the thought to her bruised heart.

She had toyed with the idea of asking the chauffeur to go on a detour in order to call to say goodbye to Doña Matilde and

Federico. There was Isabel too, but it was too late. In any case she could not ask any favour of the man by her side. I love him and I don't know what I can do about it – her eyes filled with tears as she admitted it. He had been kind, considerate and polite and, last night, even protective when she had stumbled out of the dreadful scene with Carolyn. Now it was all over.

They had left his estate well behind now and they were moving towards the hills where the air was growing perceptibly cooler as they climbed from plains to roads lined with trees. The long silence continued as the hills took on a definite shape and they swept along an avenue of trees to a square of tiny shops hiding behind shutters. Here Ramón slid in between two parked cars and shut off the engine.

He turned to her in the sudden stillness and said quietly, "We are going to refresh ourselves with a glass of wine. I am sure you are wondering what this is all about, but I shall enlighten you in due course. We have a matter to discuss and we can do so more comfortably up here where the air is much cooler. We can also talk undisturbed."

He helped her from the car and Venetia welcomed the tang in the air so refreshing after the heat of the car. She was beginning to feel a trifle feverish and found it hard to believe that she was not dreaming. It was all so strange, mysterious and unbelievable. The sense of unreality persisted as he guided her across the tree-bordered square to a quaint old tavern where he had to bend his dark head to enter.

The interior was lined with wine barrels resting against white walls and waiters moved about between alcoves of small tables serving wine. The alcove Ramón led her to was near to the fireplace at the end of the room where they would not be disturbed. Then he ordered wine.

The elderly, smiling waiter who brought their bottle of wine beamed on them as he put it down with a plate of biscuits, as if he was delighted to serve them.

It was a rich, golden wine, ice cool, and Ramón lifted his glass.

"Cheers," he said. "We have a proverb in Spain which says,

and I quote, 'If we cannot get what we like let us like what we can get.' Unquote. But more of that later.''

Dazed by overwhelming variations of feeling, Venetia sipped the cool drink warily. Alcohol on an empty stomach was something it was wise to avoid. As though reading her thoughts, he pushed the plate of biscuits towards her.

"Take a biscuit," he said, then, in the manner of a man being reasonable against his will, added in a more gentler tone, "Why did you not eat your breakfast this morning? You leave your bed much too soon after the attack of sunstroke insisting that you have fully recovered, yet you do not eat. You are even fully prepared to go on an exhausting journey with no food inside you."

Venetia picked up a biscuit. What little wine she had swallowed was bolstering her morale. The situation was intolerable. She had to end it as soon as possible. But how? There was no expression on his face. It was a polite blank. But she knew what he was thinking, his opinion of her and the situation – a cheating one – which she had been responsible for with Don Jorge. Why then was he bothering with her? Was it some sadistic streak in him that made him want to hurt her? She tasted the biscuit and the sweet almond flavour was bitter in her mouth. It was quite an effort to swallow it, for tears seemed to be blocking her throat.

"I've quite recovered, thanks," she managed evenly. "I didn't eat breakfast because I wasn't hungry."

His breath rasped in sudden anger. "You knew you were going on a journey. Surely the sensible thing to do was to eat if only a little. You really are the most irresponsible young woman I have ever known! You ought never to be let out on your own. I could spank you!"

Venetia washed the biscuit down with more wine, wishing that he would not glower at her with those black eyes. They were most disturbing.

"Meaning, of course, that I was a bad choice for the post with Don Jorge in the first place. You ought to feel happy that I'm going," she told him quietly.

He drank more wine and set down his glass with a thud. "I did not mean that at all. I was simply stressing the fact of you not being a hundred per cent fit to return to London and the cold February winds. You gave up your holiday in order to help out my uncle Jorge. The least you can do is to accept his offer to stay for that holiday at his home."

"I'd rather not. I have to go. There are things to arrange when I return home."

"What are these things you have to . . . arrange?"

"A job, for one thing."

"On the plane here you told me that you expected to be here for two years in Carolyn's place. You also asked me to say nothing about your identity to Tio Jorge. Why did you not speak the truth and admit that you were only filling in the time until your sister arrived?" he demanded.

Venetia lowered her eyes away from the dark accusing ones. "It was just one of those things that happen, and I would rather not discuss it if you don't mind." She lifted her chin militantly, her eyes reaching the firm chin and staying there in an effort to avoid his probing gaze. "I can see no point in continuing this conversation. I don't know why I allowed you to escort me on my way in the first place. You've disapproved of me from the start. I've had enough. I'm going."

She rose to her feet and instantly his hand shot out to grip her wrist painfully.

"Sit down and be quiet," he said sternly. "I have my own reasons for bringing you here."

Venetia sat down again, bewildered and taken aback, to finger her wrist which burned after his cruel grip. If he noticed the gesture he ignored it and leaned across the table urgently.

"You like Spain, do you not?" he demanded.

"I did," she answered on an awkward small shrug. "But I don't belong and never shall."

"That is utter nonsense and you know it. It only proves that you are not fully recovered from your illness. Drink your wine and have another biscuit. The morale is always low when the stomach needs nourishment." He waited for her to do as he said, but Venetia did not move, neither did she say a word. Softly he said, "Will you not do it to please me? I want to talk to you, and I cannot do so if I do not have your full attention."

"There's nothing to talk about. You and I have nothing in common." Her look was both piteous and appealing. "Don't you see it's better that I should go before . . . before we say things in the heat of anger that we don't mean. You and I have nothing in common."

He contradicted her smoothly, his eyes narrowing relentlessly. "On the contrary, we have several things in common. Drink you wine," he insisted.

"I don't want your wine!" she cried, her voice rising, but she did not care and went on recklessly, "I don't want any more of your soft soap either!"

He frowned, his face creased in puzzlement. "Soft soap?" he echoed, and added fiercely, "Is your wine not palatable?"

Venetia watched him taste the rest of the wine in his glass, torn between laughter and tears.

"I didn't mean there was anything wrong with the wine. It was a figure of speech, meaning that you're trying to coax me for some reason of your own," she told him defiantly.

"I am not trying to coax you into anything," he said sternly. "I had no intention of using the . . . soft soap. We had better begin. First of all, your sister gave Don Jorge to understand that you were returning to an excellent post in London – in short, to be secretary to her former employer. Is that not so?"

"No." Venetia compressed her soft lips together firmly, then hurried on at the sight of his raised brows. "Carolyn was not lying when she mentioned the post, but I have no intention of taking it."

"And why not, may I ask?"

"Because I don't like the man. Oh, the salary is excellent and the prospects are wonderful, but I can't stand him. He's so full of his own importance and the fact that he's one of the youngest directors on the board of the company that I would find him insufferable."

"Indeed? Have you met the man personally?" he enquired politely.

"Carolyn invited him to dinner at the flat one evening. I . . . I didn't like him. He was much too familiar."

"You do not favour men who are too familiar?"

"Not his kind. He's a married man."

"Don Jorge was married also. Did you not have qualms about working for him?" he probed.

"Not qualms about Don Jorge's integrity, only about whether I would prove to be satisfactory. Besides . . ." Venetia stopped abruptly and coloured fiercely. She did not continue.

"Besides what?" he insisted.

"Nothing."

"Oh, come, now you may as well tell me. I am curious to know why you broke off so abruptly, almost with embarrassment."

He spoke with a faint trace of humour and Venetia lifted her head to look steadily at him.

"I knew that you lived somewhere in Spain and the thought comforted me. I regarded you as an old friend . . . someone I could run to in an emergency."

He smiled, a slow smile reaching the dark eyes and filling them with a gleam that made her heart beat quicker. There was a quality in his voice.

"So you regarded me as an old friend. *Gracias*. You are making my task much easier. Tell me, what do you think of my *novia* as a person?"

His look was very searching, but his manner was friendly and relaxed.

She said honestly, "I think she's very beautiful and rather sweet. I like her very much."

"You do not find it a strain being with her?"

"No, but then I haven't been in her company long enough, have I?" she replied, wondering where his questions were leading.

He regarded her steadily, resting his arms on the table and dove-tailing his fingers.

"In a tragedy such as my *novia*'s," he began, "one tries and hopes for a possible cure. To that end I have consulted eminent specialists from Madrid to London. Some gave no hope, others that she could return to normal one day but there was nothing they could do." He spoke slowly, decisively watching her beneath the level straight brows. "After our recent trip abroad for her periodical check-up I had begun to lose hope. It is you who have again bolstered my hopes."

Venetia's heart fluttered and she gazed at him in surprise. "But why should I do that?" she cried.

"That day you went to tea with her, she was not in the least shy with you. Normally she will have nothing to do with strangers, but with you her manner was both spontaneous and happy. Remember the way she wreathed the flowers in your hair? I thought at the time that there was a strange tie of friendship binding you together. What would you say to being a kind of companion to her? I do not mean to take the place of Luisa but to be a kind of sister, talk to her, read to her, take her for walks or accompany her for car rides. I have put a car at her disposal. What do you say?"

Venetia could not say a word. Ramón picked up the plate of biscuits and offered them. She took one and nibbled it like a mesmerized rabbit and continued to stare at him. Putting down the plate, he passed a hand over the dark crisp hair which no amount of disciplined brushing could entirely keep down.

"You can think it over if you wish," he went on. "While Luisa is an excellent companion for Isabel, she is elderly and my *novia* needs someone around her own age, someone who will bring her out of her dream world into one of reality. Am I making myself clear?"

Venetia nodded briefly, in a state of stunned surprise. "I see your point. Your idea is that Señorita Valrosa has more chance of returning to normal if she leads the kind of life she led before by mixing with people of her own age."

"Precisely. I have a reason in asking for your help. Until recently I have been resigned to accept life as it is, but something unforeseen has happened, something that makes it imperative for me to act regarding my present position, and I find it impossible to go on the way I have. Everything has changed. I find my life intolerable."

Venetia swallowed the last of the biscuit, hating the look of unhappiness and a kind of frustrated longing appearing briefly on his face. She wanted to say something, anything to erase it.

"Not long ago you quoted the Spanish proverb about liking what we can get," she reminded him lightly.

Then it occurred to her that the reason for his request was not so much to hasten Isabel's recovery as it was to free him of the temptations around him. Carolyn, for instance – was she the reason for his unrest? She hardly thought it could be Chimone. Ramón had known her previously and appeared to have recovered from whatever influence she had held over him. Venetia shuddered inwardly at the future agonies in store if Carolyn was the reason for his unhappiness. Yet whatever the reason, Venetia knew she would have to go on helping him no matter what the cost to herself.

He said quietly, "I quoted the proverb for you. I knew how happy you were working with Don Jorge, and I was hoping you could be as happy with my *novia*. Your duties would not be arduous. You will be at liberty to do as you please. Luisa will take orders from you and you will find she will co-operate. She adores her charge and cannot do enough for her, like all of us. I shall insist that you dine often at the Quinta."

Venetia had taken down the rest of her wine and her hand trembled as she set down the glass. She had lowered her eyes from the appeal in his dark ones and had drunk the wine to ease the constricted feeling in her throat. It was safer to look beyond him at the fireplace with its huge flat hearth and the cavernous chimney rising above it. Maybe it was the wine on an empty stomach that was chasing her confused thoughts around her head.

To stay or go? That was the question. To stick it out grimly to the end. To see her beloved Ramón take his vows in the lovely old terra-cotta coloured eighteenth-century church of San Jerónimo with Isabel or Carolyn, then go away to live with her memories? He had said like what you can get. Very well, she would take what she could get — extra time spent near him, the chance to comfort him when he was down.

"When do you wish me to start?" she said with the sensation of having burned her boats.

His relief at her acceptance was almost tangible. "Right away. I can drive you back to the villa. But first I want you to call me Ramón. You understand, of course, why I could not address you as Venetia before. I must admit that I found it anything but agreeable to address you as Miss Mellor. Yet you gave me no other option since you were concealing your identity from Tio Jorge."

Venetia nodded. "Yes, I was very foolish. Don Jorge would think it odd when you called me Miss Mellor and addressed Carolyn by her first name."

"It did occur to me," he admitted a trifle sardonically. Then the charming smile came into play and he reached for the bottle of wine. "This calls for another drink." He refilled their glasses and lifted his own. "To you, Venetia, and to your happiness in your new appointment."

"To Señorita Valrosa," she replied, and drank.

"To Isabel," he corrected her.

"To Isabel," she agreed.

He went on to outline his plans. She was to have two complete days from her duties each week and any evenings she wished. Her salary was far too generous, but she accepted it to please him. Almost before she realized it everything was settled and they were once again in the car returning to the Quinta.

By the time they were well on their way Venetia began to feel more relaxed. At least this time she had nothing to hide and they were on first name terms, which was some small comfort. Then she remembered Carolyn. She was not going to like this. But Venetia did not care. After all, they would not be under the same roof.

Venetia felt a vague pang of apprehension when the car slid along the drive of the villa in the grounds of the Quinta. She did not know why, unless she was worrying how Luisa would react to her living at the villa. She had left as Miss Mellor and was now returning as Venetia. Then she forgot everything in her delight at seeing the villa again, so beautiful with the sky so blue and the flowers half hiding the walls. Unlike any other, it was a house in a fairy tale, and the thought of living there filled her with sheer joy.

Isabel was picking flowers in the garden. Venetia glimpsed her dark head bobbing up and down, so completely engrossed in her task that she did not see them. Then Luisa came forward with a gracious smile of welcome. Ramón, it seemed, had already acquainted her with the fact that there could be a new addition to the household. He exchanged a few words with her, then went in search of his *novia* while Venetia was taken up to her room.

Her room was light and airy, the carpet luxuriantly Persian, and vases of flowers gave a feminine touch. Luisa watched her reactions closely, her hands folded demurely on the apron of her black dress.

She said, "The Señor Conde chose this room for you because it overlooks the sea and is much cooler in the heat of the day. Should it not be to your liking you are at liberty to choose another which I shall only be too happy to prepare for you."

Venetia looked around with shining eyes at the room which was to be her own for as long as she was privileged to stay. "But this is lovely, Luisa, *gracias*," she cried. "How like the Señor Conde to have chosen a room I would have chosen myself."

Luisa nodded comprehendingly. "The Señor Conde is a very understanding man. I hope you will be very happy here, Miss Mellor."

"I'm sure I shall. I am going to do all in my power to help the Señorita Isabel to get well again," she said, adding wistfully, "Do you think I'm being too optimistic, Luisa? You see, I'm very fond of her."

"Love and faith can perform miracles, Miss Mellor," Luisa answered.

The siesta that afternoon was no problem for Venetia.

Relaxed and replete after a very enjoyable lunch with Isabel, she slept for two hours, awakening at the shrill peal of the phone by her bed.

"Hello!" said Carolyn. "Ramón has told me about your new job with his fiancée. Clever girl! How did you manage it? I didn't know you had it in you."

"I didn't," Venetia replied. "I was as surprised as you are. The offer came from Ramón after he had picked me up with my suitcases this morning. I accepted because I wanted to. I had nothing lined up back home in way of a job and it seemed the sensible thing to do."

"You could have gone home to the flat and I told Ramón you had a job in view with George." Carolyn sounded vexed.

"So I believe, but I prefer to get my own job. At least this is one you can't take from me."

There was a pause at the other end of the phone. Then Carolyn said sharply, "I didn't take the job with Don Jorge from you. It was you who took it from me, remember? Anyway, surely you aren't holding that against me? You have to agree that everything has turned out very satisfactory for you."

"And for you too. I only hope you won't put on the experienced secretary act with Don Jorge by taking over complete control. He's a pet and I wouldn't want to see him hurt. All you have to do is to type his book, nothing more."

Carolyn said furiously, "Are you trying to tell me my job? I wouldn't be so smug if I were you. You won't last there five minutes after I've finished with Ramón. I might convince him that you're the last person to be a companion to his Isabel with all your English ideas of Women's Lib!"

Venetia laughed. "Isabel is too sick to be taught anything. But Ramón is very keen for her to get well quickly."

"I can tell you why Ramón is so eager. He's found out what he's missing. He's taking me sightseeing and is planning lots of parties for me. It seems he can't do enough to repay the hospitality he received at Tamor Hall. Yes, I would say that things couldn't be going more in my favour."

Venetia's heart lurched at the underlying meaning of her

words, but she steadied her voice with an effort. "Congratulations, and the best of luck," she said firmly, and put down the phone.

Her hand was shaking when she lifted it away from the phone. Then resolutely putting Carolyn out of her thoughts, she walked across the room and opened the window shutters. The formal rear gardens of the villa meandered ostentatiously away to a low wall beyond which the sea appeared to be suspended between the blue sky and white beaches. Already she felt different. It seemed that in taking the new job she had become a happier, more relaxed person. What a lovely country it was, with the air filled with strange fragrant smells not even remotely resembling those of a city.

Nothing would have pleased her more than to know she was spending the rest of her life there. She liked everything about it, the people, the climate, the surroundings and the easy way of life, so simple yet so sincere. Here people had a respect for each other so different from England, where an inefficient government had allowed everyone to run wild. It seemed to Venetia, as she turned back into the room, that one could be very happy here.

Half an hour later, crisp and fresh in a glazed cotton dress with her hair tied back for coolness, Venetia went downstairs, to see Luisa crossing the hall en route for the kitchen to order tea.

She said, "Señorita Isabel is in the back garden picking olives for tea."

With a warm smile for Luisa who was going to make her stay at the villa so much happier, Venetia made her way to the back garden. At the back entrance she met Rodrigo, the gardener and general handyman, who, along with the help of his wife, Angelina, looked after the villa. He carried a basket of garden produce.

"*Buenos días, señorita*," he said, his leathery face creased into a courteous smile. "The little *señorita* is in the garden."

Venetia thanked him. The staff at the villa were as friendly and courteous as those at the Quinta, she thought happily, as she went in search of Isabel. They had tea on the patio and Luisa had taken away the tray when voices were heard approaching. Venetia heard Carolyn's laugh and stiffened. Then they came into view. Carolyn had her hand tucked into the bend of Ramón's arm and he was looking down at her and speaking softly.

Looking at him with her heart in her eyes, Venetia decided that he was more than handsome in the clear sunlight shining down on his black hair. There was an iron strength tempered by a rare sensitivity about his face which made it unforgettable. Carolyn looked very fair and sparkling in a white muslin dress and white shady hat.

"What a divine place this is, Ramón," she cooed, admiring the profusion of flowers that met the eye wherever one looked. Then she spoke to Venetia, who sat by Isabel on the patio. "I bullied Ramón into bringing me to see you. I never dreamed such a heavenly little place existed in the grounds of the Quinta."

Whether by accident or design, she took the vacant place beside Isabel, leaving Ramón to take the chair next to her. If Carolyn had dressed in white to create a sharp contrast to the sultry beauty of Isabel, she could not have succeeded more. Beside her fairness, Isabel glowed like a sun-warmed ripened peach. But, thought Venetia, Carolyn knew there was a surfeit of sun-warmed peaches in Spain and that Ramón might possibly prefer her own English fairness and the challenge she brought to his masculinity. He was the kind of man who would not love lightly, and his passionate nature made him very susceptible to a pretty woman.

Ramón's smile as his gaze slid over the three of them did not give anything away. He picked up the cover of the box which contained the jigsaw puzzle Venetia and Isabel were doing on the small table in front of them and after perusing it reached out to fix two difficult pieces into place.

Carolyn leaned over and made a wry grimace. "How clever of you, Ramón!" She gave a light laugh. "I do admire you for being so patient with the Señorita. You have the right companion for her in Venetia. She has endless patience and loves

116

helping people. What a tragedy to strike one so young! But one that must not have repercussions on those immediately concerned. Don't you agree?"

He set two more pieces of the jigsaw in place, then he replied, "You sound like my relatives, my dear Carolyn." He had straightened and the dark eyes were glinting sardonically. "Would it please you to look over the villa?"

"Very much. Although I don't suppose it will be as enchanting as the Quinta."

The smoothness with which he had changed the conversation did not put Carolyn out one jot. Rising to her feet, she slid pink-tipped fingers into the bend of the arm he offered and they moved away.

Venetia watched them enter the villa, shaken by Carolyn's direct attack on Ramón's defences. The bonds forged between Isabel and himself were made fast by his loyalty and, Venetia hoped, by his compassion in no small measure. This was part of the reason she herself loved him so much. Her admiration for him was two-fold, for she realised that it could not be easy for him to resist affairs with other women so blatantly offered.

Would Carolyn succeed in breaking down his defences? Just now his look had been for Carolyn alone, a fact which her astute sister would not miss. Venetia wanted his happiness so much that it alarmed her. That Isabel occupied a place in his heart she did not doubt, but how deeply rooted it was there no way of knowing. He certainly would not reveal it. As for Carolyn, the fact that between her sister and Ramón was a vague something, though undefined, was subtly apparent.

Mechanically, Venetia picked up a piece of the jigsaw and gave it to Isabel to fit into place. Maybe she was wrong and imagining things that were not there. What did she know of Ramón or his people? They were an alien race. So she argued, and came to the conclusion that her own love and deep concern for him was making her sensitive imagination work overtime. Presently Luisa appeared with a tray of tall glasses and a jug of iced lemonade. Venetia accepted a glass gratefully, for her throat was dry, and not only with the heat. From time to time she could hear Carolyn's light laugh from somewhere inside the villa and she stared out into the sparkling garden seeing Ramón's dark head bent down to the titian hair.

The jigsaw completed, Isabel wandered out into the garden to follow a butterfly fluttering across the grounds to a bush heavily laden with blossom. Watching her go, Venetia saw her own role as that of a governess for a while, not talking down to Isabel but treating her as a normal young woman. They could experiment with make-up, lightly, of course, and this could be followed up by interesting her in her clothes and appearance. Isabel was beautifully turned out. Luisa was very precise in her care, though she was apt to treat Isabel as a child, thus encouraging her in her own little world of makebelieve. Granted she was happy. Would she be so happy if she did eventually regain her full faculties? Would Ramón have become too enamoured by Carolyn by then? It was possible that he had fallen for her sister during his visit to Tamor Hall and had decided then to go back and break off his engagement to Isabel in due course. Then before he could do so Isabel had had the accident and it was too late for him to free himself honourably. This thought disturbed her profoundly and she gave a start as Carolyn's heels came tapping their way towards her.

She had taken off her shady hat to throw it on to the long low table.

"Phew, it was warm indoors!" she exclaimed, sitting into a chair beside Venetia and fanning her face daintily with her handkerchief. "That sounds refreshing."

Venetia was pouring out a glass of the lemonade and the ice tinkled against the sides of the jug.

Carolyn accepted it and crossed long slim legs. "Cheers," she said, raising her glass. "I wish you wouldn't sit there looking so cool. You're like Ramón. He never seems to mind the heat. I left him talking to Angelina in the kitchen and took this opportunity of talking to you."

Venetia did not answer. She was sipping her drink and watching Isabel in the garden.

Irritably, Carolyn said, "You're still hating my hide for cutting you out with Don Jorge, aren't you?"

Venetia answered quietly, "As a matter of fact I'm not. I'm enchanted with my new job, living in this beautiful villa and helping with Isabel. If you remember, I was taking your place and your name, an uneasy situation to sat the least, when one has something to hide. Now I have nothing on my mind and I can relax in a way I could never do before."

Her sister shrugged a trifle contemptuously. "Everyone to their taste. Frankly I don't envy you. By the way, I've been looking at the work you did for Don Jorge. You did very well."

Dryly, Venetia replied, "Thanks. I'm glad you're pleased."

"I'm starting to work with him tomorrow and I shall be free each day after lunch – an arrangement which, I believe, he made with you. Have you visited any of the cities yet, Barcelona or Madrid?"

"No. I would have got round to it eventually, I suppose, but I've been so happy in these lovely surroundings that I hadn't given it a thought. Big cities are more or less the same and I wouldn't want to visit them too often."

Carolyn took down more of her drink. "Rusticate if you want to, but I don't intend to become a cabbage. I never was the country type. Give me life in a big city every time." She spoke, slowly, thoughtfully, as Venetia waved to Isabel picking flowers. "You aren't hoping to ingratiate yourself with Ramón, are you, in looking after that demented creature?"

Venetia stiffened. "I wish you wouldn't be so callous, so lacking in understanding! Isabel has suffered an accident that could have happened to either you or me. I want to do my best for her, to help her to regain all she has lost. I hate it when you twist my good intentions into something that's against my nature. There's no reason why we shouldn't be friends. You could help with Isabel too. You'll have your afternoons and evenings free. You're welcome to come here at any time. We have a car at our disposal. We could all go to Barcelona one day."

She looked hopefully into the green eyes which did not soften. "I shall be with Ramón in my free time. He's promised to take me one day to Barcelona. You and I won't be seeing much of each other."

Carolyn's words were like pebbles dropped into a pond, and Venetia looked down into her glass. Almost unconsciously she had been hoping to see something of her sister. They could have had fun together. It was Ramón, of course. Carolyn meant to get her man. In the meantime she was taking no risks of possible rivals queering her pitch. So be it.

"You'll enjoy working with Don Jorge, but do allow him to do things his own way. Be gentle with him. If you watch him closely you'll see by his manner that he's seeking your opinion. Never force your opinion on him. His work is wholly Spanish, and therein lies its charm." Venetia swallowed, remembering the happy times she had spent with him. "You can learn a great deal from him. He's very well read and very accomplished. There are hordes of servants to attend to his needs, but don't let him go without his mid-morning drink. He's apt to overlook it when it's placed under his nose."

"Have you quite finished?" The furious undertones vibrated on the air. "You have made yourself indispensable, haven't you? When I want your advice I'll ask for it!"

Carolyn put her glass down with a thud on the table and Venetia said wearily, "Don't forget you gave me a whole lot of advice on how to be the perfect secretary to your last but one employer. I didn't resent it – what I resented was being pushed into a job I didn't want. I would have been grateful for it in different circumstances. But you've never been grateful for anything, have you? You've always wanted more."

Suddenly Carolyn was shaking with laughter. "You really are funny, almost pathetic in your consideration for others. Carry on and see where it gets you. And if you mean I should be grateful for Julian, you're wasting your time in reminding me."

"I never mentioned Julian. The fact that you have means that he's there at the back of your thoughts. So there's hope for you yet."

They both looked up as Isabel approached with her arms filled with flowers. For a moment she stood before them shyly, then thrust them at Carolyn.

She was equal to the occasion. "Why, thanks, Isabel. It's very kind of you," she said, accepting them.

"What a pity I haven't a camera with me or, better still, that I'm not an artist to take down this enchanting picture before me for posterity. Such charming scenes are rare. A bevy of beauty!"

Ramón was standing on the patio of marble tiles and alabaster pillars half hidden by a lovely profusion of trailing blossom. The sun burnished his teak tan and emphasised the whiteness of his smile. Carolyn had risen, eager to be gone yet pausing in the knowledge that, with the flowers clasped to her breast like golden sunshine, the scene was wholly hers. No man with red blood in his veins, and Ramón had plenty, could resist a beautiful woman for long.

With this thought in mind, she cooed sweetly, "Your little *novia* is delightful. I must buy her a present when I go to Barcelona. I hope it will be soon. You did promise to take me, Ramón?"

She smiled provocatively up into his narrowing gaze.

"You do not like it here? You are bored?" he demanded.

"Oh no!" Her laugh jarred on Venetia's sensitive ear. "I just don't want to miss anything. Besides, no one could explain the wonders of your lovely country better than yourself."

Venetia's heart quivered. She looked at the completely oblivious Isabel, at Carolyn's cajolery and Ramón's intentness which could only mean one thing – his desire to please.

After a brief consideration, he said, "We are dining this evening with my aunt and uncle who are leaving this weekend along with Chimone to attend a house party in Barcelona. Perhaps you would like to accompany them?"

Carolyn hesitated, for once at a loss. This was something she had not expected. However, she rose to the occasion with a flashing smile.

"I scarcely know them, Ramón. It would be different if you were to come too. Do you mind if I think about it? I'm in no hurry to go," she murmured.

"Not at all."

For some reason Ramón's lighthearted mood seemed to have evaporated. He took his leave with Carolyn, patted Isabel's head and gave Venetia a brief nod, leaving her behind to stare after him curiously.

That evening after dinner when Isabel had gone to bed, Venetia took her Spanish phrase book with her on to the patio and tried to study, but after a while she gave it up, for the night sounds were too new and distracting for her to concentrate. Somewhere in the garden a nightingale was singing and she closed her book to sit back and listen to the clear, pure notes. This evening they held a kind of poignancy, as if the little bird was singing because he was lonely like herself. She thought of Ramón and Carolyn dining out, sharing an intimate car ride together, and decided that studying Spanish grammar gave one little time for disturbing thoughts. She was opening her book again when a figure suddenly stepped into the light of the patio.

Don Jorge looked taller than usual and very regal in the evening cloak covering his evening suit.

"*Buenos dias*, Miss Mellor," he greeted her courteously. "You do not mind my calling on you? No doubt the hour is late for a visitor according to your English standards. For us in Spain half the night is our day."

"On the contrary," she assured him with a smile closing her book, "I'm only too pleased to see you. Do sit down."

He sat down beside her to face the garden, leaning forward to tap the tube of ash from his cheroot into an ash tray on the table confronting them.

"You do not mind if I smoke? I see you have an ash tray but no cigarette."

Venetia shook her head. "I smoke very little," she admitted. "How nice of you to call."

He leaned back in his chair, content to enjoy his smoke and the beauty of the night.

"How are things with you, my child? You are very brave to come to reside with the poor Isabel. Does the very thought of it not dismay you?"

Venetia shook her head. "Why should it? Isabel is a sweet girl and I like her very much. I'm going to do my best to get through to her. How was she before the accident? Do tell me about her."

"She was a happy, normal young woman. Ramón would not have become engaged to her otherwise." Don Jorge paused and seemed to continue with reluctance. "I do not approve of my nephew asking you to come here. He is a man of strong principles and strength of purpose. Yet even a man such as he, at the top of his form both physically and mentally, cannot will the young woman back to her normal self."

"Probably not, Don Jorge. Yet surely you admire him for trying? It's a terrible position for him to be in," Venetia said gently.

Don Jorge looked very wise. "*Gato con guantes no caza ratones*," he quoted slowly. "Which translated means, 'A cat in mittens catches no mice'. My nephew's hands are tied while he insists on finding this cure for his sick *novia*."

The words hung ominously in the still night air and Venetia turned her head slowly to see the truth in the fine old eyes. That Ramón should waste his manhood on Isabel was to Don Jorge a great tragedy and one that he deplored.

Don Jorge studied the end of his cheroot. "Ramón has a godlike position here at the Quinta. The estate covers vast acres of land which he has cultivated to the highest degree. His vines make wine of an excellent quality, his olives are the finest in the land, his goat's milk the creamiest and his fruits the plumpest. Acres of barren land have been made arable through his endeavours and he has built a hospital and a school for his workers. All this he has done to forget his own desires of the heart, desires which can beset a man of deep feeling – for a wife, a family."

The bitterness of his tones revealed only too clearly his deep affection for his nephew. He went on heavily.

"His *novia*'s illness has not affected her because he has surrounded her with loving care and devotion, denying to himself the fulfilment of his manhood. He owes it to himself

123

and to his estate to marry and produce an heir."

"Which I am sure he wants to do with a clear conscience," Venetia spoke in defence of her Spanish grandee with a mixture of pain and admiration.

Don Jorge smiled sadly. "Maybe I am getting too old to share your optimism." He patted her hand. "But do not forget, my child, that a starving man can only go on so long."

Venetia was still pondering over that last remark with increasing misgiving when, later that evening, she prepared for bed. Was Don Jorge thinking along the same lines as herself regarding Carolyn's arrival at the Quinta? His old eyes would not miss her sister's blatant advances to his nephew. Maybe he was all in favour of Ramón marrying an English woman, since it would be better than him not marrying at all.

During that quiet hour she had spent with him on the patio, Don Jorge had not referred once to his book or the manner of her leaving his employ, and somehow she had never plucked up enough courage to mention it. Maybe it had been because he had really seemed to enjoy that quiet smoke in the cool of the evening as he had unburdened his mind. The envelope had been there on the low table on the patio when he had gone. Venetia had never seen him put it there.

She had opened it with trembling fingers to see a cheque for services rendered, her salary for the short time she had worked for him. Her lips trembled and her eyes clouded over at the thought of a gesture made to save her any embarrassment by not giving it to her personally. Nice person, Don Jorge, nice people the Spanish, she had thought, blinking back the sudden rush of tears.

She went to sleep that night wondering where it was all going to end.

CHAPTER SEVEN

VENETIA'S first week at the villa was a happy one with an early morning bathe offering breathing space in which to take in the enchantment of her new life. Immediately upon wakening, she would leave her bed to put on a swim suit and towelling robe. From her window, the sea was an inviting, placid blue part of an ever-changing landscape patterned by deep violet shadows changing to indigo, then palest blue as the daylight grew stronger. Stealing through the silent villa, she could hear Angelina singing softly in the kitchen. Rodrigo, her husband, was already at work in the garden and he would call out a greeting to her and add a remark about the weather in his quick, decisive Spanish.

On reaching the beach, Venetia shed her towelling robe to wade into the water, gasping a little when the waves closed over her with a cool sharpness that was stimulating. She swam hard for a time, each stroke clear and decisive as though she knew where she was going. Maybe she did. She would forget Ramón and concentrate on the task in hand. He wanted Isabel to recover so that would be her goal. She would help the poor girl assiduously to come out of her shell, meet young people of her own age whom she had known in the past and little by little, lead her back into the world she had shut herself away from. She would emulate her in every way.

Venetia knew that when eventually Ramón went his way, she must then go hers. One had to adapt oneself to life one way or another, however hard it proved to be. Whether or not she would be hurt in the process was something she did not think about. She must live for the moment and allow the pleasures to carry her through the sadness. At the moment, swimming strongly through the caressing waves, she felt fit enough for anything, fit enough to will Isabel back to life and Ramón. When her muscles began to pull, she floated on her back revelling in the peace and serenity of her surroundings.

On her fourth morning at the villa, Venetia was plodding up the beach after her swim when a scene she had witnessed the previous evening returned to taunt her. Before going to bed she had taken a stroll in the garden, walking down as far as the low wall at the rear overlooking the beach. A huge orange sun slipping down behind the horizon had presented a scene of flame and gold silhouetting trees and hills into dark cut-out shapes.

Leaning on the stone wall, Venetia had suddenly been struck into stillness by the sight of two silhouetted figures moving slowly along the edge of the water. There had been no mistaking the outline of that dark arrogant head, those wide shoulders, as Ramón moved with looselimbed grace beside the familiar figure of Carolyn. With her heart beating in thick, slow strokes Venetia had watched them stand to look over the water for what seemed an age. She had no idea if they had been talking, they had been too far away for that, and presently they had retraced their footsteps back to the Quinta.

The fact of Carolyn strolling at night without a chaperone in the company of a man would not cause comment at the Quinta. The women from Inglaterra did odd things, and that was one of them. Left alone with thoughts becoming more unbearable with every moment, Venetia had hurried back into the villa. Venetia had refused to dine at the Quinta that evening because Isabel had not been well. Since coming to live at the villa, she had discovered that Isabel had attacks of migraine and was apt to become violent until given a sedative prescribed by the doctor. Luisa dealt admirably with her charge on these occasions, keeping them secret from Ramón because they were of short duration and Isabel was perfectly all right upon awakening after the sedative. The attack of migraine had come on suddenly when they had returned from paying a call on a friend of Isabel's for afternoon tea. When Venetia had enquired about Isabel's friends, Luisa had told her of two of them, a young Spanish woman recently married who lived but an hour's car ride away and an unmarried one who lived about the same distance.

Venetia had ordered the car put at their disposal by Ramón

and they had driven to pay a call on them. At first, Isabel's friends had been rather silent and uncertain what to say. It had been left to Venetia to lead the way and in the end they had been chatting and treating the silent Isabel normally. Their visits had been brief, just afternoon tea, but Venetia had come away more than satisfied. Her next move would be to invite Isabel's friends to the villa. She had planned to talk it over first with Luisa before asking Ramón's permission, but now the attacks of migraine had presented a new problem, since Isabel would only reveal them by acts of violence.

On their return to the villa, Venetia had left Isabel with Luisa and had gone to her room. She was about to dress for dinner when there was a cautious tap on her door. Luisa stood there, pale and shaken.

"Come to the Señorita's room quickly, please," she whispered urgently.

She followed Luisa into Isabel's room and leaned back against the closed door, utterly astonished. Isabel was pummelling the bed with her fists. She was lying full length across it, burrowing her head into her pillow. As Luisa had made her way to the bathroom returning with a glass of water and a capsule in her hand, Isabel's movements had increased in violence, her hands and feet drumming frenziedly on the bed. Luisa put down the glass on the bedside table, sat on the bed and turned Isabel over on her back. Then, forcing open her mouth with a finger and thumb on her chin, she put the capsule on the back of her tongue and closed her lips together. Her movements were swift and sure, firm yet gentle, as she thrust an arm beneath her charge to raise her head and set the glass to her lips.

There was the sound of teeth against the glass, then Isabel was gulping part of the water down her throat. At last she had sunk back on the bed exhausted, to lie quiet and still while Luisa bathed her swollen face and pushed back the black hair from a hot forehead.

Venetia had stood transfixed with surprise and compassion. The poor child looked so forlorn and vulnerable that she had to blink back the tears. Isabel was asleep before Luisa had undressed her to put her to bed. As she carried on with her task, Luisa explained.

"I had to let you see the Señorita in one of her attacks so you would know how to cope if I was not available. The capsules are kept in a cabinet in the bathroom. I will always leave you the key if the need arises. You will promise not to tell the Señor Conde when you go to dine with him this evening?"

Venetia leaned back, grateful for the support of the door. This was something she had not expected, but she would surmount whatever difficulties arose from it.

"I shall not be going to the Quinta this evening without Isabel. I shall telephone to say we're much too tired to go out after an exhausting day spent visiting friends."

Luisa looked worried. She had looked after the Señorita Isabel since she was born and it would break her heart to be parted from her. This was the real reason she had not told the Señor Conde of the migraine attacks, fearing that he might be influenced, on hearing about them, to send her charge to a home. He would be very angry indeed if he were to find out. He would never have sent Miss Mellor to the villa. If Miss Mellor did no longer want to stay, she, Luisa, would understand, but please not to tell the Señor Conde what she had seen that evening.

Venetia hastened to reassure her. "Your secret is safe with me, Luisa. We can share it together. Thanks for telling me. I shall stay, of course. It will make no difference. I would have come had I known about the migraine attacks."

The scene faded from Venetia's mind as she left the beach and walked through the quiet gardens. She had been much too numb last evening for it to register clearly, which was probably why she had taken it so calmly. However, there was to be no drawing back. Whatever the outcome she was right in the middle of it.

Isabel came down to breakfast once more her silent, docile self. Indeed, Venetia began to wonder if the incident of the previous evening had been a dream, a figment of her own imagination brought on through her own complete absorption in her surroundings. But Luisa's smiles and nods in her direction made it true enough. Sharing a secret had somehow brought them closer together.

It was after the siesta that Luisa came to knock on Venetia's door.

The Señor Conde was downstairs. He had come to take the Señorita Isabel and herself to a picnic. Would she please to get ready. Venetia, on the verge of stretching luxuriously after her rest, became suddenly very wide awake. Luisa had gone before she could ask if Carolyn was with him. She would be, of course. Hastily, she took a shower, put on a polka-dotted muslin dress, floating and summery, and trod into white sandals. Then cramming a white straw hat on her hair and taking her shoulder bag, she was ready.

She reached the patio to find Ramón sitting at the small table, a cheroot in his hand and a drink at his elbow. He was alone. Inevitably their eyes met and she felt a leap of her pulses.

"Ah, *buenos dias*, Venetia. I am flattered not to be kept waiting. You look refreshingly cool. Spain seems to agree with you. She puts extra lights in your hair and the eyes are bright and clear." His quick warm smile was evidence that her appearance pleased him. "Do sit down while we wait for Isabel. How are you? Rested, I hope, after your exhausting time of yesterday?"

To her annoyance, Venetia felt the hot colour rise to her cheeks beneath his mocking regard. She sat down not too near him and put her bag down on the floor beside her.

"Yes, thanks," she told him warily. "We went to visit friends of Isabel's. We have made two such visits, and both were so enjoyable that I want your permission to invite them here to the villa."

He blew out a line of smoke from his cheroot and narrowed his eyes.

"Who are these friends?" he asked, and leaning an arm on the table regarded her intently.

She told him and he nodded, quite pleased. "I know the families very well, and I see no reason why you should not invite them to the villa. The newly married young woman you went to see married an old suitor of Isabel's. The young woman's parents were disgusted when Isabel's parents turned him down in my favour."

"But why?" she said.

He tapped the ash from his cheroot into an ashtray on the table.

"Because he is wholly Spanish and I am not. My mother was English. She died when I was born, and my father never married again. It seems the menfolk in our family love only once."

His eyes and lips, slightly amused, acknowledged that he understood the sympathy she had not voiced.

Venetia dropped her eyes beneath the intensity of his gaze. She saw the old yellow tiles of the patio like beaten gold in the slanting rays of the sun stealing beneath the arches, sombre and rich, and her heart reached out to him because he had never known a mother's love and she prayed inwardly that life would be kind to him. All the riches in the world could not make up for all that he had missed.

Isabel appeared looking sweet in coffee lace and silk with matching shady hat on her dark hair. Ramón put them both in the car, Isabel beside him, Venetia in the back, and they were off. The drive through the estate took quite some time and Venetia stared out at familiar scenes until the car began to climb. Now and again, she gazed at the back of Ramón's wide shoulders and wondered where Carolyn was. Then resolutely she kept her gaze ahead as the car dipped and they descended to go through a village of white houses with grilled windows and small picturesque shops where Ramón had to slow down almost to a stop to avoid the children and goats which seemed to abound in the narrow streets. Some of the villagers recognised the car and called out greetings to him which he acknowledged with a dazzling smile and a lift of the hand before winding his way up narrow twisting streets to the main road. They negotiated a bridge and the landscape grew softer, greener. Green fields sprinkled with tiny delicate flowers between rocks and boulders lined the road where trees gave shade.

Ramón ran the car on to a grass verge and turned off the engine. At this altitude, the air was cool and sweet with the scent of jasmine and wild honeysuckle. Venetia and Isabel followed Ramón, who carried the picnic basket to the shade of trees where tall boulders formed convenient backrests and they sat down.

The picnic basket was opened and the spread was mouth-watering, ice-cold drinks in flasks, a bottle of wine in a wicker basket, home-cooked ham in wine, newly baked crusty bread, farm butter, fruit and cheeses. Venetia felt happy to the point of lightheadedness. Ramón's nearness, his teasing dark eyes, his fingers touching her own when he handed her the food filled her with a joy that brought a flush to her cheeks and a song to her heart.

They had returned to the villa and Venetia's joy took a final bow when Ramón said as he helped her from the car, "I leave tomorrow for Barcelona with Carolyn to spend the weekend with relatives. Should you wish to contact me while I am away, Don Jorge will give you my phone number."

Late that evening Venetia had retired to her room after a short walk in the grounds of the villa feeling not the least sleepy. She had put on a wrap and was combing her hair when a discreet tap came on her door.

Carolyn stood there with a coat over her evening dress. She whispered urgently, "I'm glad you haven't gone to bed. Can I come in?"

She moved gracefully into the room and watched Venetia close the door behind her.

"Take a chair," Venetia said. "I thought you'd forgotten I existed. To what do I owe the honour of this visit?"

Carolyn sat down and loosened the coat on a wave of delicate perfume as she did so. Her smile was ingratiating. "I've come to ask a favour. As for calling to see you, I have to work until lunch, as you know, and I believe you've been out most afternoons paying social calls. I saw the car one day. You passed when I was in the village of Santa Marta."

Venetia had moved to lean back against the dressing table. "Who told you we've been paying social calls?" She lifted a hand. "I know – Rosa, the maid. What is this favour? Has it anything to do with going to Barcelona tomorrow?"

Carolyn, who had been placing the folds of her evening dress as it spread around her, looked up sharply. "How did you know I'm going to Barcelona?"

Venetia eyed her calmly. "Ramón told me this afternoon."

The green eyes narrowed thoughtfully. "So that's where he was! How long has this been going on?"

Venetia kept a steady look as her sister produced a packet of cigarettes from her jacket pocket and lighted one. Her eyes moved to the smooth white column of Carolyn's throat as she threw back her head to keep the smoke from her eyes.

With deepened colour and angry eyes, she said, "How long has what been going on?"

Carolyn laughed. "Venetia, you needn't try to hide it. I know the real reason why you took this job. You're in love with Ramón – it sticks out a mile. But it won't work. I can see you've mistaken his courteous attention as meaning something more." Her eyes hardened, became bright like polished emeralds. "I'll never believe that he'll ever prefer you to me."

Venetia, pale with anger now and disgust, said bluntly, "You would never believe anything. It didn't occur to you, did it, that Ramón would be sure to call on his fiancée from time to time, as he has always done?"

The jealousy was hardly restrained. "How many times has he visited you? Every morning, no doubt, while I was busy working with Don Jorge?"

Determined to keep quiet about the picnic, Venetia said coldly,

"As a matter of fact he hasn't been near since the day he brought you to the villa until that afternoon. I was rather surprised that he hasn't called before."

Carolyn's smile was smug. "No doubt Ramón has been working hard in the mornings in order to be free to take me out in the afternoons. At the same time he wants to do the right thing by Isabel, which is why he engaged you to keep her company. He doesn't feel so bad at neglecting her himself now that he knows you're there to keep her company." The thick tube of ash on her cigarette prompted her to gaze around for an ash tray which was thrust out to her from the dressing table.

"Thanks," she said coolly. "Where was I? Oh yes. You will let me know if Isabel begins to show any sign of returning intelligence, won't you?"

Venetia's fingers curled around the edge of the dressing table. Her heart lurched, bewildered at the obvious satisfaction in that smooth, hard voice.

The words were hard to say and her lips trembled on each one. "Has . . . has Ramón . . . discussed the matter with you?" she asked weakly.

Carolyn laughed outright. "What you mean to say is, has he made love to me, isn't it? Didn't you know that a Spaniard makes love first with his eyes? Surely you expected it? Or were you counting on your new job luring him to your side?"

Venetia quivered as each word from those smiling lips jabbed at a sensitive spot. But she was determined not to quarrel. She said quietly,

"Ramón is not wholly Spanish. He had an English mother – or didn't you know?"

The quick look of surprise confirmed that she didn't. Carolyn was, however, quick on the uptake. She waved a careless hand. "Which explains why he goes for English girls. Don't you see?"

"I can see that you've joined forces with Ramón's relatives to badger him into putting Isabel in a home."

"My dear Venetia, there's no question of my badgering Ramón, as you so delicately put it. You needn't be on your high horse about something which doesn't concern you. Ramón is in love with me all right. I know the symptoms. He's in at the deep end, believe you me. Why should he send for Julian if not to tell him that he plans to marry me?"

Venetia stared. "But why send for him? Why not write or something?" She cleared her throat. "Does he know about you and Julian having some kind of understanding?"

Carolyn shrugged. "Ramón evidently has some bee in his bonnet about Julian and myself and wants to do the honourable thing. He asked me for Julian's address."

"And did you give it to him?"

Another shrug. "What else could I do? I didn't mind when I realized why he wanted it. I shall have to work quickly to persuade Ramón to propose to me before Julian arrives. You know how tiresome Julian can be where I'm concerned? Which brings me to the reason I'm here." Her smile was friendly. "I want to borrow your Spanish shawl. We're to stay with some cousins of Ramón's in Barcelona. There's also an old aunt who will no doubt look me over. I suppose Ramón wants her approval of his future bride, and the shawl will give the old girl the idea that I'm conforming to Spanish life."

Venetia went to open a drawer in the dressing table to take out the Spanish shawl lovingly wrapped in layers of tissue paper and put it down gently on the bed.

"I'll find a bag to put it in," she said, gazing down at the heavy gold fringe protruding from the wrappings. "It's lovely, isn't it?" Her voice was wistful. "As you say, it's just the thing for you to wear in Barcelona."

She found a good sized plastic bag and dropped the shawl inside.

"There you are. If you carry it by the handles it won't crush it."

Carolyn was on her feet in a trice, grabbing the bag eagerly after putting out her cigarette.

"Thanks. I'll do the same for you some time. When I'm married to Ramón I shall be in a position to do favours for you – even find you a husband."

She moved towards the door, pulling her jacket around her, as Venetia winced inwardly, torn between wanting her to go and wanting her to stay. Somehow she did not want to be on her own just then. Besides, she wanted to hear about Don Jorge and his book.

At last she asked, "How are you getting on with Don Jorge?" Her smile was tender, recalling her pleasure while working for him. "He's a pet, isn't he?"

Carolyn paused with her hand on the door knob. Her answer came offhandedly.

"He's all right, I suppose. I haven't your capacity for deep emotion. He doesn't say much. In fact he talks very little."

Venetia's eyes widened in surprise. "That's odd. He was always talking to me. He has a wonderful sense of humour. I hope you aren't working him too hard?"

The answer came pat. "That fact that I go through three times as much work as you apparently does mean I'm more efficient, that's all. I suppose it will seem like rushing to you because I'm more experienced."

Venetia shook off the sting with a sad shake of her head.

"You don't understand, do you? Those memoirs are Don Jorge's baby, to be nursed along gently, to chat about them as he goes on. He doesn't have to stop at intervals to pop a pep pill into his mouth to keep him going like that executive boss of yours. Don Jorge lives naturally, happily. We English have forgotten how to."

"Very touching!" Carolyn's laugh was derisive. "Really, you're so romantic that it hurts! You would be just right for Julian. He has sickly sentiments like hanging on to his estate when he could make a fortune carving it up into plots of building land. You should get together."

The next moment she had gone, leaving her perfume to taunt.

CHAPTER EIGHT

VENETIA sat on the patio, drowsy and comfortable. Today her siesta in her room had been restless, so she had cut it short. She had been the first to appear from the slumbering household. The sky was a perfect blue, with everything slumbering in deep shadows covered by a shimmering haze. Luisa's knitting lay on one of the white wicker chairs and everything was still.

The car drew up silently with the sun dazzling on the black polished roof. Venetia sat up instantly awake to see Ramón's chauffeur, Miguel, slide out of the driving seat to open the car door for Don Jorge.

"*Buenos dias*, Miss Mellor," he said politely, his dark eyes above the small neat beard, twinkling down at her. "I am indeed fortunate to find you alone."

He looked tall and distinguished in his cloak with his silver-knobbed cane held at an angle emphasising his air of dignity.

Venetia was on her feet instantly, pulling forward a chair and placing the cushions comfortably for him.

"Don Jorge!" It was impossible to keep the pleasure from her voice. "Do sit down while I go to the kitchen for a cool drink for you." Her mouth curved sweetly, conspiratorially. "Have you been naughty and cut short your siesta like me?"

He sat down and placed both his hands on the knob of his stick planted firmly on the ground between his feet. Then he said darkly, "Neither of us appear to be any the worse. Indeed, may I say that you do very well on so short a siesta. There is a cool transparent delicacy about you which I find infallibly endearing."

Venetia laughed, a small tinkle, absurdly pleased that she was fresh from a shower and was wearing a white sun-dress with blue motifs on the breast pocket and around the full skirt.

"I'm sure you haven't driven to the villa just to pay me compliments," she told him with a smile. "What kind of a drink can I get for you? Iced lemonade? A sherry?"

He waved a delicately boned hand. "No, no. I came to collect you."

Venetia sank down on to her chair in surprise. "To collect me?" she echoed.

"Yes, my child. What do you say to coming home with me to spend the weekend with Doña Matilde and Federico?"

Her sudden gasp was one of pure delight. "I would love to."

"Then go and fill a weekend case. Miguel will fetch it."

"Now? This minute?"

"This minute."

She gazed at him with shining eyes and parted lips feeling strangely lightheaded. Then she sobered.

"What about Isabel?" she asked.

Don Jorge leaned forward and patted her hand as it rested on the arm of his chair.

"You have earned a short respite from your charge and I am sure Luisa will be the first to agree with me. Now go and pack that case while I have a word with Luisa."

Venetia gazed through the car window to see the mountain peaks piercing the blue sky. She sat in the back of the car with Don Jorge. Miguel was in the driving seat, his wide shoulders enhanced by the smart uniform of Ramón's household. His peaked cap was set rakishly on black curls, a young man with a roving eye for the ladies, especially for Venetia, so it seemed. His bold glance had lingered on her slim form appraisingly and his fingers had deliberately touched her own when he had taken her weekend case to carry it downstairs to the car.

But Venetia did not mind. It was all part of a wonderful day of boosting her morale. She was going to see Doña Matilde again and laugh at Federico's absurd compliments. For the past hour she had been conducting a conventional conversation with Don Jorge, pausing now and again to admire the passing scenery.

"It's all so grand, so awe-inspiring," she exclaimed enthusiastically. "A truly wonderful place to grow up in."

Don Jorge turned to look at her glowing face. "Yes, there is a lot to be said for growing up in a healthy environment," he agreed, studying the youthful curve of her cheek as she gazed out of the window. "Do you like it so much?"

"Oh yes!" she breathed, leaning forward to look at a windmill and oxen ploughing a field.

"What do you plan to do when your work with Isabel is over? She might recover and get married. Either way I cannot see you keeping the job indefinitely."

"I ... I haven't given it a thought," she stammered.

Suddenly she was thinking about it and was shattered at the thought of leaving the Quinta for ever.

"You could marry while you are here?" he suggested kindly.

She shook her head. "I don't think so."

His eyebrows lifted at her heightened colour. "I have embarrassed you and I apologize. You must forgive me. I did not mean to probe." He paused as if choosing his words. "I was prompted by my interest in your welfare. While your sister has that self-assurance that will carry her through a successful career, you are very different. You have the excellent qualities of making some man a fine wife. You have deep emotions capable of great and lasting love, while your sister is more materialistic in her outlook on life."

"Carolyn is very efficient in her job. She works very hard," Venetia felt bound to say something in defence of her sister and she looked tentatively at his closed profile.

He seemed to think this over. Then he said thoughtfully, "I would agree that she does very well in her job in London where the tempo of life is much quicker than it is here. While it is good to be so efficient, some men like to conduct their business affairs a little more leisurely." He lifted a blue-veined hand with a gentle smile. "Do not misunderstand me. It is merely that I find your sister's drive a little wearing."

Venetia could think of nothing to say to this and he went on,

"However, she is enjoying herself. Ramón has several things laid on for her entertainment. After their weekend in Barcelona he is having a house party. Doña Matilde and Federico are to return with us to stay at the Quinta with other guests."

Venetia's heart went cold. "Are the celebrations for some reason?"

His shrug was very Spanish. "The usual country festivities. At one time the Quinta was always filled with guests until the tragedy of the Señorita Isabel cast a cloud over everything. I live in hopes that it may soon be lifted."

And what then? Venetia closed her eyes. She had not the courage to think that far ahead.

As if by mutual consent they lapsed into silence. Don Jorge had closed his eyes and leaned back his head. The journey seemed to be never-ending with the drone of the car engine lulling her into sleep as the light faded. She was jerked awake by the swerving of the car entering the courtyard of the Villa Allicia. They had arrived. Venetia stumbled stiff-legged and weary from the car with Miguel's grip of her arm hardly registering. Then Doña Matilde was greeting them, embracing her father, her words tumbling out Spanish fashion in her delight.

"How are you both? Did you have a good journey? You did? But so exhausting!"

Venetia felt all the warmth and sincerity wrapping around her like a cloak.

"We have missed you both so much." Federico had come forward. "Now it seems you have never been away."

They sat for a long time on the patio that evening after dinner enjoying the cool night air and talking into the small hours. Venetia was drooping with fatigue, but like Don Jorge, she knew her company gave pleasure to Doña Matilde and Federico. She had to thank Doña Matilde again for the lovely Spanish shawl and answer her questions about Carolyn, saying how lovely she was. No mention was made of Carolyn taking her place with Don Jorge, for which she was thankful.

Don Jorge was the first to go to bed, followed by Doña Matilde who wanted to make sure all preparations had been made for his comfort. Venetia was about to follow suit when Federico laid a hand on her arm.

By now Venetia was very, very tired. Her eyelids refused to stay open and a yawn was lurking ominously around her jawbone. The journey and the wine taken at dinner were having their effect. She wanted her bed, but even as she told herself this, the expression of Federico's face bade her stay.

"Please stay a while," he begged. "I will not keep you long. I know you must be tired. The staff are all in bed, so I am to see to everything for the night. More wine?"

"No, thanks, Federico."

Venetia folded her hands in her lap and waited.

He had walked to lean back against one of the alabaster pillars supporting the patio to present a serious profile.

Talking to the courtyard, he said, "How is Isabel?"

"A little less inhibited, I think. We have been visiting her friends this last week and she appears to enjoy it. I do wish there was some way of getting through to her." Her voice was full of feeling as though by sheer will power she would make Isabel right again. "I gave her your present, but I don't think your name registered."

She saw him wince and began to understand as he turned his head slowly to look at her.

"You have guessed I am somehow involved with Isabel?" The bitter pull of his mouth acknowledged her unspoken reply, and he went on, "Isabel and I have known each other all our lives. She was a close friend of my sister before she married, consequently we saw a lot of each other. I knew that some day I would marry her, that there would never be anyone else for me."

He dug his hands into his pockets, tight-lipped and unhappy. "She was only eighteen and I was still at university when I was told a marriage had been arranged between her and my cousin Ramón. I was shattered. When the accident happened I was glad." His nostrils dilated. "Glad because Ramón could not have her, the woman I loved more than he."

He looked so distinctly alien in that moment that Venetia felt drawn into depths she had not known existed. She shivered in the half peaceful, half barbaric night, at the same time seeing in him a fellow sufferer from unrequited love.

"I understand," she said gently. "I know you don't mean that. If you love Isabel as deeply as you admit to doing why don't you take part in fighting for her recovery?"

The fire of passion had gone from Federico's face, leaving it blank.

Venetia leaned forward eagerly. "If you've been so close to Isabel it is possible that you're the one who can get through to her."

"How, precisely?"

"By being with her when you can, showing her old photographs taken when you were young together. Don Jorge says you're going to be guests at the Quinta. You'll be seeing her there."

He said hoarsely, "Do you know what you are asking of me?"

"Yes," she told him calmly. "I'm asking you to help to get Isabel back to her former self, whether it's to marry the Señor Conde or not. What is to be will be."

"*Fatalista!*" Federico's mouth twisted into a sneer. Then he laughed. It was not pleasant.

Venetia's face grew hot. "I beg your pardon. I thought your love for Isabel was an unselfish love. It seems to me that your feeling for her is nothing more than jealousy of your cousin. *Buenas noches*, Federico. I'm tired."

His face flushed too with anger, and he moved quickly to tower above her before she could rise to her feet. Silently she looked up into his working face, aware of a sense of conflict, of something within him battling for freedom but as yet unresolved.

A muscle worked in his cheek. "I am sorry, angel, please forgive me. You are right." His slow smile told her then that his ardour, his power to give through his love, matched her own. His eyes narrowed down at the fairness of her upturned face, the aura of tawny hair, her luminous eyes, the soft pink lips slightly parted. "At this moment you appear to me like a Botticelli angel come to bring me my heart's desire."

"It's the magic of the night," she replied teasingly. "There's no need to pay me extravagant compliments. I think it's time we went to our rooms."

They smiled into each other's eyes with a deeper understanding. On their faces was the knowledge that they were fighting for a lost cause, the result of which could be the beginning of life for Isabel.

"There is one thing I want to say before we part. You, my angel, are the only one I have ever confided in regarding my love for Isabel. Not even my mother knows."

Venetia nodded. "I understand, Federico. I'll respect your confidence. Your secret is safe with me. *Buenas noches.*"

Venetia's visit to Don Jorge's home was an enjoyable and relaxing one. Federico was his usual gay self and only Venetia saw the pain behind the smile. They returned to the Quinta on Monday around four in the afternoon. Venetia travelled with Don Jorge and Miguel with Doña Matilde and her son following in his car. Miguel dropped her off at the Villa and continued to the Quinta with Don Jorge, who was tired after the journey and regretfully refused to stay for afternoon tea.

Doña Matilde and Federico stayed, and the meal was a gay one. Venetia ran to find Isabel, who was sitting in her room staring out of her window at the sea. She hugged her and gave her some of her favourite chocolates in a pretty box tied with pink ribbon. Isabel hugged her in return and the tears came into her eyes in her delight on her return. Her affectionate greeting after a weary journey cheered Venetia and made her all the more determined not to give up hope of her eventual recovery.

After tea Doña Matilde and Federico were leaving for the Quinta when the long black car slid up behind Federico's almost without sound. Federico had kissed Isabel's hand and was bowing over Venetia's in his usual clowning way when Ramón slid out of his car, straightened and took in the situation at a glance.

"*Buenas noches*, Tia Matilde, Federico. I take it you are on your way to the Quinta," he said smoothly, flicking a glance at Venetia's hand still held in Federico's grip. "May I present Miss Carolyn Mellor, sister of Venetia?" He turned then to Carolyn, who was seated in the front seat of his car. "Carolyn, may I present Tio Jorge's daughter, Doña Matilde, and Federico, her son."

Carolyn, looking bandbox-fresh in a green suit the colour of her eyes, extended a gloved hand through the open car window and while greetings were taking place, Ramón moved to Venetia to look down at the faint shadows beneath her eyes.

"You look tired, Venetia. You are well?"

Her expression was as noncommittal as his. His unexpected appearance had not only shaken her but had also revealed the depth of her love for him. She still loved him, more than ever. There was nothing she could do about it except hug the knowledge to herself in silent misery.

Her smile was pale. Her voice husky as she pulled herself together.

"I have been to Don Jorge's home for the weekend. We arrived back at four and Doña Matilde stayed for tea with Federico."

He looked down at her, loose-limbed, eagle-eyed and impervious to the heat, and said slowly, "Did you enjoy it?"

"Very much. You didn't mind my going?"

He frowned. "Why should I? You are free to go where you will. You are not tied down to set hours. I am giving a dinner this evening at the Quinta when most of the guests will be there who will stay for most of the week. You are invited, but not Isabel. She would be embarrassed and not a little alarmed at the number of guests. As you will not be expected before nine o'clock, you will have ample time to rest."

Had he infused a little enthusiasm into his invitation, Venetia would have accepted like a shot, but as it was, she was repelled and bewildered by his manner. Something had upset him, and she wondered what it could be.

Pride came to her aid and she lifted her chin to speak with perfect calm. "If you will excuse me, I would prefer to stay at the villa. I am tired. Besides, Isabel will be disappointed if I don't have dinner with her this evening."

"As you wish." He gave a slight bow as if that was the end of it. He had made no attempt to persuade her to change her mind. Oddly enough he did not look at all happy. In fact he did not look anything except that he was already regretting inviting her to the Quinta. "*Buenas noches*," he said formally, and she answered in the same vein.

He went then to have a word with Isabel, who stood with Luisa in the background. Then, with his long economical stride, he made for his car, slid into the driving seat and lifted a negligent hand. The sun glinted on the roof of the car as it shot away, followed by Federico and Doña Matilde, and Venetia was left with the memory of Carolyn's smiling face framed in the car window as she waved victoriously.

Venetia awoke early the following morning, as is the case when the mind is beset with problems, and lay for a long time watching the dawn light stealing into the room. Maybe she had been wrong to stay so near to Ramón after discovering her love for him. Love had come unasked and, while she had been far from happy at the pain it brought, she had accepted it.

Carolyn's smile at the window of his car had implied that her weekend in Barcelona with Ramón had not been disappointing. Ramón's curtness could have been the result of the restraint he had put upon himself when Carolyn had set herself out to charm.

Poor Ramón! After all, he was not married to Isabel and one could not blame him had he accepted the kind of comfort and momentary contact he craved from Carolyn. Venetia sighed and, refusing to think any more, left her bed and put on her swimsuit.

Angelina singing in the kitchen and Rodrigo greeting her from the kitchen garden did much to lift her depression. Then the warm, buoyant water was washing over her limbs and by the time she was shrugging into her towelling robe, she was feeling much better. Pushing back her swiftly towelled hair, she was picking up her beach bag when a movement far away to her right riveted her to the spot. With a fast beating heart, she told herself that Spain was filled with wide-shouldered, black-haired men and this one could be a guest from the Quinta enjoying an early bathe. But that familiar loose-limbed walk, the arrogant poise of that dark head, could only belong to one man.

In a sudden panic, she was all for ignoring the hand he lifted in greeting as he drew nearer, and the urge to run was hard to suppress. However, one did not openly ignore an employer, especially in Spain, where courtesy was as natural as breathing. So she waited. And there he was, looking down at her, vibrant and glowing, his hair still damp from his recent dip in the sea. He was now fully dressed in the usual immaculate suit, one hand thrust into a pocket with careless elegance.

"*Buenos días*, Venetia." His voice was rich and deep on the clear morning air. "Last evening you were exhausted, but this morning you are full of energy. I am pleased to see it. I would like to talk to you. Shall we sit on those rocks there?"

He indicated huge white boulders a distance up the beach in flat and tall shapes. He had obviously been there before, for he led the way to a kind of armchair hewn in the rock and she sat down. He remained standing leaning back nonchalantly against a tall pile of rock a little to her right and presented her with his profile as he gazed out to sea. The silence, broken only by the soft lap of the waves on the beach, seemed interminable. Venetia longed to say something bright and witty, but found it impossible to say a word. All she could do was to draw her wrap more closely around her and assume a calm expression.

He began, "When I asked you to take the post of companion to Isabel, Tío Jorge was dead against it. He said it was the wrong kind of post for you, that Isabel needed someone a little less sensitive, someone who would not be emotionally involved as he was sure you would be. I told him he was wrong, that you were very fond of Isabel and would regard her as a beloved sister."

Venetia traced the black vein running through the marble rock serving as an arm-rest with a finger that was not quite steady. "Are you trying to tell me that you don't want me any more?" she said.

"Want you?"

His voice sounded strange, as strange as their meeting in the early dawn light. It occurred to her then that he must have been up very early to have already bathed in the sea and dressed. Had he been awake all the night? Was his need for Carolyn making it impossible for him to rest, torn as he was between two fires? He looked lean and fit, tanned to a permanent degree which went so well with the black hair and black eyes. He also had hordes of Spanish servants to attend to his every need. Why had he stopped talking, and why did he not turn his head to look at her?

He did. She felt rather than saw him turn slowly to look at her and she was thankful for the silky curtain of hair half hiding her downbent profile.

He continued, "I am in doubt whether my plan was a good one after all, especially as your sister Carolyn remarked about your tiredness last evening. She suggested you could be feeling homesick."

Venetia stiffened. So her dear sister was not content with taking her job away, she now wanted her out of the country. But why? Carolyn had never been so vindictive before. She had always enjoyed a clear run with her own boy-friends. Venetia had never presented herself as a rival whenever Carolyn had a boy-friend to supper. Why, then? Was she afraid of Isabel regaining her normal intelligence too soon?

Indignantly, she said, "I came out here of my own free will perfectly content to stay for a period of two years. Does that suggest to you that I am homesick?"

She lifted a face with a blob of angry colour on her cheeks which deepened as she recalled the manner of her coming, the little act of deceit in covering her own identity, which she felt this infuriating man beside her would always hold against her.

He smiled slightly. "Remembering your enthusiasm over the beauty of my country, I must confess I thought this most unlikely. However, I had to be sure how you felt. Do you find being with Isabel too much for you?"

Venetia clenched her hands. "What I am supposed to say to that? I love Isabel, and since I've been here at the villa, I'm prepared to do everything I can for her, not only with equanimity but with a wholehearted compassion. Does that answer you?"

"Thank you," he answered quietly, and was again talking to

146

the sea. "I'm more indebted to you than I can say at the moment. Something has happened recently, something of the utmost importance to me as a person. Like the proverb, I have trained myself to like what I can get. Now I want something which, at the moment, I cannot get in the present circumstances, and I am going through a kind of refined torture which some day I hope to explain to you. I am telling you this because I want you to accept things which you may find difficult to understand." He paused, then added, "Am I making myself clear?"

Clear enough, she thought, to know that it was Carolyn who was putting him through his own little private torture, Carolyn who had been clever enough to dig inside his armour and reveal the man. The pain in her heart was excruciating and suddenly it seemed to be mixed up rather oddly with the pain in her foot. Looking down, she saw to her horror that a swarm of king-sized ants were running madly over her sandals, and when a particularly vicious stab was directed at her ankle, she cried out and tore off her robe.

The next moment she was running madly down to the water, stopping only to clear the sandals frenziedly away from her feet. Only when she was wading knee deep in the water did she again draw breath. Oh, the relief when the horrible creatures were no longer on her skin! Ramón stood on the edge of the water examining her sandals, her wrap thrown over his shoulder, her beach bag on his arm.

"All clear," he said, looking concerned. "You had gone before I realized what had happened."

His look of concern deepened as he saw her quivering as he helped her into her towelling robe.

"Poor child, you are shocked," he murmured rather thickly above her ear, and drew her gently into his arms and moving a hand soothingly over the back of her head as it lay against his chest. "Try to relax. There is nothing to fear. They have gone."

Venetia closed her eyes and went limp against him. Her heart beat heavily against her chest wall, vibrating into him as she stood crushed against him. His arm was like an iron band about her squeezing the very breath from her lungs and she was sure he was not aware how tight he was holding her.

He was speaking again into her hair. "I would not have had this happen for all the world. Had I not brought you to sit on the rocks it would not have happened. I am deeply sorry, Venetia."

Slowly she gathered her scattered wits. His voice sounded odd and not at all like him. She was not feeling like herself either and the pressure of his arm was becoming unbearable.

Her voice came at last, muffled against his chest. "Don't ... blame yourself. It ... it was my fault entirely. I ... I shouldn't have panicked the way I did. But they were ... so big ... and there were ... so many of them. I ... I was terrified."

"I know. They are vicious little creatures. Just relax."

When, at last, Venetia summoned the strength to draw away from him, she was breathing quickly but had subdued her agitation.

He looked straight down at her. "All right now?"

She nodded, mustering a smile. "Yes, thanks."

After a swift appraisal of her pale face, he was down on his knees, wiping her slim golden legs and the sand from her feet with the towel taken from her beach bag. Then he was putting the sandals on to her feet.

"There," he said, looking up at her with a faint smile. "There are none of the little brutes in your sandals. I have examined them. We must be thankful that the little demons leave only a red spot."

He patted her leg reassuringly and was on his feet again with the alert movement of active muscles.

"Sure you are all right?" he insisted.

She nodded. "Perfectly."

With nerves stretched and quivering, Venetia jerked the girdle of her beach robe around her slender waist. Then she flung back her head to smile at him reassuringly.

"Honestly," she said. "Please don't worry about me any more."

His dark eyes met hers unwaveringly. He had taken her wrist

and was noting her pulse. His touch, his nearness was transmitting all kinds of electric currents through her body. She had never felt so vulnerable, so close to revealing her inmost feelings.

It occurred to her then that she was staring up at him with tremulous lips and eyes. Her senses were swimming and, although his next words were like a douche of cold water, Venetia never ceased to be thankful at the brake they put on her emotions. He had been bending his head nearer and nearer to her parted lips. Then, just as she was sure he was about to kiss her, he said with narrowed eyes, "How remarkable. With your hair falling back from your face, so, you are the image of Carolyn, your sister." He straightened and touched the tawny hair lightly with a finger. "Strange I had not noticed the likeness between you before."

Perceptively, he withdrew to present his previous image, that of her employer. His voice, a little thick at first, was now even and cool to match the expression upon his face. Agonizingly, Venetia told herself that he was so besotted with Carolyn that he was seeing that lovely face in her own.

Her bright smile concealed the agony in her heart. "A certain expression perhaps," she answered flippantly. "It often happens in families."

In that moment she would have given anything to have been in Carolyn's place.

He nodded, his face enigmatic. What had brought about his sudden withdrawal, his closed expression, she would never know. He had cast aside that habitual cool front miraculously for her, and it had now dropped again. Maybe Carolyn was the only one who could dismiss it altogether.

"Sure you are feeling all right?" he insisted.

She dropped her eyes from his disturbing perusal of her pale face and nodded. He was taking this as a dismissal and, handing her the beach bag, was moving away when she succumbed to an uncontrollable desire to keep him with her a little longer.

"I'm sorry," she said. "I never asked how you'd enjoyed your visit to Barcelona. Did you have a nice time?"

Some of the grimness left his face. He smiled, a tight smile and said softly, "I would not have missed it for anything. A truly remarkable visit and one I found to be most stimulating."

One had to be quick to catch that mocking gleam flashing fleetingly in the dark eyes, but the implication of his softening was clear enough to Venetia. Something important had happened during the weekend in Barcelona, a serious talk with Carolyn, an exchange of vows, meaning only one thing. He had made up his mind at last about his future wife. It could only be Carolyn.

She forced herself to act normally under the blow as he bowed over her hand courteously.

"*Buenos dias*, Venetia, until this evening. Federico will be calling for you at eight. I am giving a ball at the Quinta for my guests. Take a warm drink when you return to the Villa, a sweet one, good for shock. I shall ask Luisa if you have done so. Take care of yourself."

Her smile as she echoed his "*Buenos dias*" had the tang of tears.

CHAPTER NINE

VENETIA shook out the folds of her evening dress, the eau-de-nil silk chiffon she had worn with the delightful Spanish shawl, and it occurred to her then that Carolyn had not seen fit to return it after borrowing it to go to Barcelona. Not that it mattered. She still liked it, but the thought that Carolyn had worn it in Ramón's company, that she could have been wearing it when he kissed her, had taken the joy out of possessing it. She would wear the white nylon fur stole.

She was ready when Federico called for her, and his look of admiration more than made up for the loss of her shawl.

"With my cousin's compliments," he said, presenting her with a cellophane box containing a spray of orchids. "May I?"

Rather sadly, Venetia watched him take the delicately veined flowers, so cool, so elegant, from the silver-lined box and fasten them upon her dress. She hated to think of them wilting in the heat of the ballroom and would have loved to keep them in the cool moss of the box because they were from Ramón.

The ball had begun when they reached the Quinta. The hall banked high with flowers was empty except for the occasional footman bearing covered trays as they hurried across the exquisitely tiled floor shining beneath the lights like beaten gold. Music guided their footsteps beneath arches to the ballroom, exciting and colourful with the moving mass of dancers. With Federico it was easy to enter unobtrusively and make their way on the edge of the dancers to a sheltered alcove where Doña Matilde, looking lovely in a midnight blue gown, sat waiting for them.

"Here she is, Madre," Federico said to his mother. "Is she not beautiful?" He seated Venetia next to Doña Matilde and audaciously kissed her hand. "I had to keep a firm hold of her on the way here in case she disappeared up a moonbeam!"

Venetia laughed with Doña Matilde as a waiter hovered and Federico presented her with a glass of wine.

"Flatterer," she said. "Fairies don't drink wine."

"But they do, the wine from cowslips," he answered unabashed.

Suddenly Venetia was surrounded by young men eager to dance with her and she was whirled away, leaving Federico to dance with his mother. On her way round the room she caught sight of Carolyn who looked radiant in a dress of sea green chiffon. Rhinestones sparkled at her ears and throat and she looked radiant.

She had circled the floor before she saw Ramón. He was standing on the fringe of the dancers, his black head lowered to listen to an elderly, plump woman whose corseted figure had again assumed the elfin grace of her youth beneath his unfailing charm. His smile was slow, showing excellent teeth, and brought that familiar twitch to Venetia's heart as he led his companion on to the dance floor.

After that, her evening was filled with a succession of partners with Federico vainly trying to keep her to himself. Ramón had been similarly occupied with Chimone, who had been talking to him coquettishly in her rapid Spanish as they passed, then several more elderly dowagers and their daughters before dancing with Carolyn. They had made a striking couple and more than Venetia's head had turned to watch them circle the room.

At the interval, Federico had brought her refreshment and left her to go to see if his mother was similarly supplied. It was Don Jorge who came to sit beside her at the little table in the alcove before Federico returned.

"Can an old man thrust himself upon you now that your watchdog is away?" he asked, unabashed. "I enjoy dancing, but the interval is a sign that I have enjoyed an elegant sufficiency. The older one becomes the more one prefers a cheroot to most things. My bones are not what they were. One of the advantages of old age is that you can sit and watch others make fools of themselves." He chuckled. "Do I sound cynical?"

Venetia echoed his chuckle. "If you do you can't hide the fact that you are enjoying yourself," she answered. "How are you?"

"All the better for seeing you. May I say how very enchanting you look in that very pretty dress?" He lighted a cheroot and his old eyes twinkled as they met hers in a query.

She nodded consent. "Go right ahead and enjoy your cheroot," she said, wondering at the meaning behind his lightly spoken words as he sat back in his chair to inhale blissfully. "Federico has gone to see if Doña Matilde is all right."

He nodded. "She is with a little barrel of a man who is paying the usual absurd compliments. She has the blush of a young girl on her cheek."

Venetia chuckled. "How nice! You Spanish males are very glib with your compliments."

"Compliments are an important part in the art of courtship. The *señorita* of one's choice is beseiged with compliments by a suitor in order to soften her heart towards him. They are often spoken in the presence of a *dueña*. That is the Spanish way."

"I gathered that. I suppose you find our ideas far too advanced to your own."

He nodded. "Fortunately, we understand and accept your way of life, as we hope you will accept ours. No doubt you saw Ramon leave the room just now to walk in the garden with your sister? Had he behaved so with a Spanish *señorita* his action would have been construed as a declaration of love to all present."

A cold hand closed around Venetia's heart. "Perhaps it is," she suggested wanly.

He did not contradict this, but took his cheroot from his lips to gaze at it thoughtfully.

"It is left to one to conjecture and form one's own opinion. Ramón is a closed book these days. He has become very preoccupied, even touchy. One wonders what has wrought the change."

Venetia sipped her wine and nibbled at a pastry. Ramón had been closely watched by his friends and relatives for years. Now they were conjecturing about his association with Carolyn. Venetia could not say in truth what she thought about it at this stage. If he wanted to marry Carolyn that was his own affair. As for herself, she loved him enough to put his happiness first.

It was as simple as that.

Swallowing the rest of her pastry, she said reassuringly, "No doubt you will know in due course of his intentions. I'm sure he appreciates your concern, especially as the burden he carries is so great."

"The burden is of his own choosing."

Venetia looked at the proud profile. "Yet you would have admired him less had he not faced up to his responsibilities."

There was a long pause during which Don Jorge leaned forward and tapped the ash from his cheroot into an ashtray on the low table confronting him.

"You are right. But I wish he would settle the matter one way or the other."

He spoke heavily and she felt the weight of his unhappiness where his nephew's future was concerned.

"I shouldn't worry about it." Venetia smiled to cover her own heartache. "Your nephew is master of his own destiny. He is free to do as he chooses and I'm sure he will make the right decision in the end."

Don Jorge's dark eyes were razor sharp beneath the beetling brows.

"Ramón is indeed fortunate to have such a loyal and charming friend in yourself, so wise for one so young."

Venetia felt something stir in her heart as the old eyes met her own. Was it possible that he had guessed her secret? His bland smile, however, gave nothing away. He graciously lifted a hand to pat her own.

"Thank you, my child," he said warmly. "It is a a case of the young comforting the old. At this moment you are very Spanish inasmuch as you have a serenity and a demure sweetness so pleasing in our own women. We must find you a Spanish husband."

His absurdity made her laugh. "Now, now, Don Jorge," she teased him. "Who is paying the compliments now, and I have no *dueña* with me."

He chuckled, raising his eyes above her head. "No, but you have your host standing right behind you. You have come at a most inopportune moment, Ramón. I was enjoying my talk with Miss Mellor. Now, as the interval is over, you have no doubt come to ask her to dance?"

Venetia's breath caught in her throat. She was aware of nothing save the man standing behind her. His sudden appearance was so unexpected and swept her away so surely from the tranquillity she always enjoyed in Don Jorge's presence. She quivered as he spoke.

The deep brown tones vibrated above her head. "Since I have not yet had the honour, my dear Tio Jorge, is it so surprising?"

Don Jorge shrugged goodhumouredly. "I am surprised that you have not asked our very pretty young friend to dance before."

"Then I suggest I do so immediately." Ramón moved from behind her chair to give a slight bow. "Will you do me the honour, Venetia?"

He offered his hand and, placing her own into it, Venetia rose to her feet. Before she could conjecture as to how much he had heard of their conversation, she was in his arms. The music obliterated sound and laughter around her until only her heart beat audibly in her ears like the crash of cymbals. Her dress billowed out against him and his wide shoulders shut out the other dancers. She did have a glimpse of Chimone, who looked at her very guardedly as she passed. Then Venetia gave herself up to the pleasure of the dance. They did not speak, and she closed her eyes. That was her mistake. She should not have closed her eyes and made her senses more acute, more aware of his own special brand of masculine fragrance – the scent of tobacco mingling with after-shave lotion emphasising his essential maleness. Her whole being began to ache with a need of him and she opened her eyes to meet his intent gaze.

The music was petering out on the dance number and he whirled her to the open archway of the ballroom. Slowly his arms released her.

"Thank you, Venetia. I enjoyed that immensely," he said quietly and gravely. "We must repeat the pleasure later." He consulted his wristwatch. "I have arranged for a cabaret at ten. There is time for you to go to see if your sister Carolyn has recovered sufficiently from her headache to come down to see it. I sincerely hope she will. She will enjoy it."

Venetia came down to earth with a jolt. While he had been talking, she had stared up at him stupidly, trying to take in what he was saying.

"Of course." Her forehead puckered into a frown. "You say Carolyn has a headache? It's most unusual for her. I'll go to her at once."

Turning swiftly away, she collided into Federico, who was obviously coming in search of her.

"My angel!" he cried, holding her arm longer than was necessary. "I have been looking for you. The cabaret is starting soon and I. . . ."

"Ah, Federico," Ramón's voice cut in smoothly. "I may need your help in that direction. Venetia is going to her sister who is indisposed at the moment."

With a chilly inclination of his head to Venetia, he strode away, leaving Federico to stare after him. His white smile had disappeared behind a slight frown of disappointment and he raised silky eyebrows to look down at Venetia.

"Is your sister ill?" he queried. "She seemed gay enough before the interval?"

"A bad head," Venetia answered laconically. "See you later, Federico."

Rosa, the maid, was leaving one of the rooms along the spacious corridor on the first floor. She waited for Venetia to reach her and smiled courteously.

"Miss Mellor is not in bed. She has a slight headache," she vouchsafed, and held open the door for Venetia to enter.

The shutters were open and moonlight streamed into the room with an unearthly radiance, shining softly on the delicate colouring of richly brocaded elegant furniture. Carolyn was standing at the window and turned at the sound of voices at the door.

"Oh, it's you," she said ungraciously.

"Who were you expecting, Ramón?"

Venetia advanced reluctantly into the room. It was clear that

Carolyn was in one of her moods and she was wishing she had not come. Bitter experience had taught her that there was no shaking her out of them except by leaving her alone.

"How is your head?" she asked, sitting down on one of the tapestry-upholstered chairs.

Carolyn gestured angrily. "I have no bad head. It was pure invention, an excuse to lure Ramón out into the garden. Do you know how many dances I've had with him all evening? Two." She walked to the dressing table to pick up a packet of cigarettes in shaking fingers and apply a lighter to one of them.

Venetia watched her throw back her head to blow out a thin line of smoke towards the ornate ceiling.

"What did you expect?" she demanded. "The man has to look after his guests. As a matter of fact he must be concerned about you, since he sent me here to ask if you feel up to coming down to the cabaret. He's anxious for you not to miss it."

Carolyn sat down on the bed broodingly. "Then he can come up and fetch me," she snapped. "What chance have we to be on our own in that crowd? All those dark hooded eyes following us around like TV cameras when we were dancing together! It's so frustrating when I know it's only a matter of time before Ramón proposes. Otherwise why did he take me to meet his relatives in Barcelona?"

Venetia bit on a soft lip, conscious of her own blistering pain.

"Why be so upset about it," she said quietly, "since you're so sure of him? Chimone, for one, will be very pleased if you don't show up for the cabaret."

Carolyn treated the idea of Chimone as a rival with contempt by ignoring any suggestion of it.

She hit the bed with her fist. "It's this business of Isabel that's holding him up." Her look at Venetia was baleful. "You could do something about it if you wanted to."

"What do you mean? I could? What on earth can I do?"

"You could talk to Ramón about Isabel. He'll listen to you."

"What about?" Venetia looked vacant.

"For goodness' sake don't be so obtuse! You know what about. Look, I've committed myself to work for two years with

Don Jorge. All right. It might sound a long time, but at the rate I'm going I'll never bring Ramón to propose even in that time."

Venetia eyed her soberly. "Aren't you rather rushing things?"

Carolyn looked fit to explode. "Rushing things, with Julian coming? He could be on his way right now."

"Oh, I'd forgotten about Julian," Venetia admitted honestly.

"Oh, you had?" Carolyn's sarcasm was marked. "I wish I could forget about him coming. Now you see why I'm so worried?"

Venetia nodded. "What do you want me to do about it?"

"Tell Ramón that you can't do anything for Isabel, that you're going back to London. Try to persuade him that she would be better in a home among her own kind."

Venetia was horrorstruck. "You must be mad to even suggest such a thing! It would not only be downright cruel but dishonest too. Besides, what gives you the idea that Ramón will listen to me when I tell him what his relatives have been telling him for the past five years?"

"He'll listen to you. He has faith in you or he wouldn't have engaged you to look after his fiancée."

"Maybe I was his last hope. He's pretty desperate for her to show some signs of recovery. A drowning man clutches at a straw."

"Exactly." Carolyn took her up eagerly on this. "That's what I mean. A few well chosen words from you and he'll give up hope and take your advice. Don't you see?"

Venetia said slowly, "I can only see that you're more desperate than he is to resort to such lengths to get what you want." Her eyes were fixed on the tube of ash hanging perilously from Carolyn's cigarette. Rising swiftly, she grabbed an ashtray from the dressing table and thrust it at her. Then she sat down again weakly in her chair. "You would do that to the man you're going to marry? I can't believe it," she breathed.

"Don't look so stricken." Carolyn tapped the ash on to the ashtray and tried to look reasonable. "Can't you see you would be doing him a favour? Besides, I like him very much. He's a real man, and how many do you find these days like him?"

Venetia quivered inwardly. To her there would never be anyone remotely like Ramón in her eyes. She wished hopelessly that he was poor, then Carolyn would have let him off the hook long ago.

She swallowed on a painfully dry throat. "Ramón has engaged me to do my best for Isabel and I'm going to do just that. What kind of a marriage can he have with Isabel always in the background of his thoughts? Count me out of your scheme. You're on your own. You're trying hard to be rid of me as well as Isabel – you're trying very hard. You told Ramón I was homesick and hinted at my tiredness the other day."

Carolyn's mouth fell open and a guilty flush stained her cheeks.

"I was concerned about you. I didn't ask him to send you home."

Venetia shook her head. "Perhaps not in so many words, but the intention was there. You can't fool me, Carolyn. I know you too well. Ramón's no fool either." Wearily, she rose to her feet and turned to walk towards the door. "Are you coming or not?" she demanded. "You'll get no help from me."

The ashtray was put down on the dressing table with a thud and there was the sound of a compact clicking open as Carolyn repaired her make-up.

"I'll follow you down. I won't forget this!" The compact clicked shut. "No, wait, I'll come down with you. Ramón could be waiting for us."

Venetia never remembered much of the cabaret. Her party spirit had gone in a wave of tiredness. Ramón met them in the hall to escort them into the ballroom where all the guests were assembled at small tables around the edge of the dance floor. They sat down, Carolyn deliberately placing herself on the centre of the three vacant chairs leaving Venetia and Ramón to sit each side of her.

At the end it did not surprise her in the least when Carolyn suggested to Ramón that they should accompany her through the grounds to the little Villa. Desperately tired and craving solitude, she walked with them, allowing them to do most of the talking, and refused to think of them walking back alone to the Quinta. At the door of the Villa she slipped away from them swiftly into the silent interior.

Some day it would be as though Isabel's tragedy had never been, as though Carolyn and herself had never gone to the Quinta or Spain. She was thinking this as she crawled into bed to fall asleep with exhaustion of the spirit.

Mid-morning, Federico came to the Villa with an album of photographs taken of himself, his young married sister and Isabel when they were children. Luisa went to fetch refreshments and Federico sat between Isabel and Venetia on the patio to show them the album. The last part of it was filled with photographs of the three of them in their teens. Each time he came across a photograph of himself, Federico would show it to Isabel, then gesture that it was a photograph of himself. Each time he came across a photograph of her he would do the same. She watched him solemnly with no sign of recognition in her big dark eyes, but she did take the album from him when they had gone through it and refused to give it back.

"Let her keep it for the present," Federico said in an aside to Venetia. "It might do some good if she continues to look at it."

He stayed to lunch. When he had gone, Venetia went to her room for the afternoon siesta wondering where it was all going to end. On her dressing table was the orchid Ramón had sent the previous evening. She had popped it into water after taking it from her dress. She touched the waxen petals gently and remembered with a pang that she had not thanked him for it.

That evening there was to be a carnival in the village of Santa Marta. The guests from the Quinta were going and it had been arranged that Federico should take Venetia and Isabel in his car. Ramón's party had been given seats on the balcony of the Town Hall overlooking the village square. There was to be a procession of fancy dress and tableaux through the streets and Ramón was to present prizes to the winners at the end of it.

To Venetia driving to the village was pure enchantment.

Sunlight sent a golden glow over the quaint little shops slumbering behind their shutters and the small neat houses with their façade of flowers from iron balconies looked as they had done centuries ago. Nothing had changed. They had refreshments on a balcony above the main party from the Quinta. A table and three chairs had been set for them. Immediately below Venetia could see Doña Matilde seated with Ramón, Carolyn and Don Jorge, while to their left Chimone sat sedately with Ramón's aunt and uncle.

A band playing in the square gave a festive air and soon a murmur from the crowds lining the streets gave warning of the carnival procession approaching. Six flamenco dancers came first to perform a fantastically swift dance to the sound of castanets. They were followed by people in fancy dress and tableaux, some religious, others depicting the fruits of the seasons.

Venetia, leaning over the balcony rail with Isabel, had thoroughly enjoyed it. It was Federico who suggested that they should leave before the streets became congested with revellers. Dancing, singing and the drinking of wine would go on through the night and he had orders from Ramón to get them away early. He was to take Isabel back to the Villa and Venetia was to go on with him to dinner with the guests at the Quinta.

Venetia took away with her a picture of Ramón with the sun turning his dark hair to ebony as the charming smile flashed up to them with a gesture of a brown hand. It was unbelievable that she should be so in love with him after being so casual with men friends in the past. It was far more shattering than she had expected. She could even begin to envy Isabel for her serenity and freedom from anguished thought. The only pain she knew was from her migraine, poor child.

Federico had taken them to his parked car via the back of the building and then they had sped away, leaving the village and the sound of merrymaking far behind them. Tenderly, Venetia looked at Isabel sitting between herself and Federico. Suddenly her heart lurched. Isabel was behaving oddly. Her fists were clenched and she was gritting her teeth. There was no doubt about it that the noise of the carnival had possibly vibrated on her poor bewildered brain to bring on a migraine.

Before Venetia could gather her scattered wits, Isabel flung out her arms and caught Federico at the side of his head, and the car lurched madly. Someone screamed and Venetia knew no more.

She opened her eyes to gaze up dazedly at the vast expanse of sky. She was lying on her back with her arms outstretched on something cool and soft as a bed – grass. Gingerly, she moved first one leg and then the other without pain and gradually pushed herself up into a sitting position to find that she was all right. She was on the grass verge at the side of the road. Federico's car was some distance away, apparently untouched and standing on the left-hand side of the road.

There was no sign of Isabel or Federico. The road was empty with not even an odd donkey in sight. She tensed at the shrill cry of a bird flying overhead and listened to the sound of swiftly running water in a gully behind her beyond the trees. Slowly, apprehensively, her eyes were drawn again to the car to see a dark head appear suddenly above it. It was Federico.

There was blood on his forehead from a cut and he drew a handkerchief from his pocket to wipe it dazedly. Then he made his way towards her like a drunken man.

"Are you all right, angel?" he asked hoarsely. "*Por Dios!*" He sank down beside her and covered his face with his hands, the handkerchief against his eyes. Numbly Venetia listened to the storm of Spanish pouring from his lips and she shivered in the warm air.

"What's happened?" she cried. "Federico, pull yourself together. I had no time to do anything. Isabel had an attack of migraine – that's why she flung out her arms. What's happened? Tell me?"

He told her then that the car had somersaulted to the other side of the road and landed on its wheels. Venetia's door had been flung open and she had been thrown on to the grass verge. Both Isabel and himself had struck their heads, but he had managed to drag her from the car. She now lay on the grass in

162

front of the car, which was why Venetia could not see her. I took him some time to say that she did not seem to be breathing.

Instantly Venetia was on her feet. With the strength of panic, she was gripping Federico's wrist and urging him to his feet.

"Come on, quick! I won't believe she's dead – not after what she's gone through. Come on, we've got to do something!"

Everything had happened so quickly, like a nightmare, that it was only when Venetia dropped on her knees beside Isabel that she realized how much her legs were trembling. She had to clench her teeth to stop them from chattering together and she prayed silently for calm. And as she gazed at the unconscious Isabel, calm came. She lay like a lovely Spanish doll flung there by some childish hand. Her eyes were closed and there was no sign of a bruise or any marks upon her lovely, serene face. Rigid now, almost holding her breath, Venetia placed a thumb on the fragile wrist.

Sweat oozed on her temples, yet her hand was icy cold as she sought for a pulse beat. In that eternity of time she ceased to think. Her face was compressed into a mask of stony concentration. She was galvanised into activity with a grim determination to infuse life into the apparently lifeless figure before her. Then she felt it, a faint regular beat that brought the tears of relief rushing to her eyes.

"She's alive, Federico!" she gasped, seeing him through a mist of tears as he dropped down on his knees beside Isabel. "Talk to her, Federico. Say anything, only keep on talking. If anyone can get through to her, you can."

The soft words of endearment were spoken in Spanish. Federico was doing more than talk to Isabel. He was kissing her all over her face, tasting the salt of his own tears as they fell. For a long time there was only the sound of his voice. Then a moan came from Isabel's lips, so faint that Venetia was not sure she had heard it. The next moment the thick heavy eyelashes trembled and parted and the big, dark eyes were looking up into Federico's. For what seemed an eternity they continued to look at each other. Isabel's eyes were no longer blank. They mirrored conflicting emotions of bewilderment and anguish as her memory returned. And with it came her voice, trembling but clear.

"Madre! Madre?" she cried. "Federico, I cannot waken her. Help me!"

Convulsively, she clung to him to break into a storm of weeping. The years had rolled back for her to the time she had found her mother prior to her fall downstairs. The blow she had received minutes ago had moved something back into place. Venetia rose to her feet to leave them together. They had already forgotten her as Federico spoke soothing words. Venetia said a silent prayer of thanks asking for Isabel's recovery to be a permanent one.

It was much later when they all climbed back into the car. Federico joyously inspected the engine, announced all was well, and Isabel sat between them looking, to outward appearances, just the same. But she had received a blow on the head, Venetia thought, and the doctor must be summoned without delay on their return to the Quinta.

When Venetia had left them alone together after the accident, Federico had told Isabel all that had occurred after her blackout resulting from her fall all those years ago. Now she turned with great surprise to Venetia.

"You are Venetia who has been helping Luisa to look after me," she cried. "And you, Federico, called me back when I was going to join Madre. Those tears you shed were all for me. Dear Federico! My prince kissing me awake."

Federico looked grim. "You already have a prince. Ramón is your *novio*. Remember?"

But Isabel only smiled and she reached up a hand to touch the gash on his forehead where the blood had congealed. "Your poor head! I shall bathe it."

Poor Luisa was overcome when Isabel greeted her on their return. The doctor arrived and examined Isabel but could not account for her miraculous recovery. Apart from the bump on her head she was unhurt. He examined Venetia, pronounced her unharmed, and put plaster on Federico's gashed head. Then, after another searching look at the radiant Isabel, he muttered something about a miracle and took his departure, promising to call again the next day.

Neither Venetia nor Federico went to dinner at the Quinta that evening. Venetia asked Luisa to send a tray up to her room. As she told Federico, Ramón would be there soon and they would have much to talk about. She reminded him that he must put Isabel's happiness before his own and he promised to do so.

She sat by her window that evening to eat her dinner. Luisa brought it up, full of her dear Isabel. She seemed to have shed years. Her sallow face and dark eyes glowed. Really, she did now know whether she was on her head or her feet. The Señor Conde was there, and somehow the news had seeped up to the Quinta to bring his relations to see for themselves if it was true that the Señorita Isabel had recovered. The salon downstairs had been full to bursting. And now the Señor Conde had sent them all away back to the Quinta, anxious that his *novia* should not be too confused after her dreadful experience with the car. Later, there would be the wedding to see to. Fortunately, the Señorita Isabel had her wedding dress and everything put away. She was to have worn her mother's dress and Luisa could see no reason why she should not do so.

When she had left the room Venetia ate her dinner full of thought. While she was as happy as Luisa at Isabel's miraculous recovery, she could not overlook the fact that her own days at the Villa were now numbered. It had not been easy for her to stay in her room instead of being downstairs joining in the elation pervading that overcrowded salon. Far less easy had it been to resist meeting Ramón again. It would take years to tear him out of her heart, if ever she did. One thing was certain – she could not stay for the wedding, not now, with the pain so acute and her love for Ramón eating her heart out.

She was lingering over her coffee when the peremptory tap came on her door and her heart dipped in her breast as Ramón entered. He was across the room in two strides to look down on her searchingly. "*Buenas noches*, Venetia," he said, eagle-eyed. "How are you feeling after your unfortunate accident? Doctor Fontera assures me that you have suffered no ill-effects, but I cannot believe it. You could easily have been . . ."

He broke off suddenly and moved to the window where he stood for several seconds before turning round to face her. His expression was not clear, standing as he was with his back to the light.

"You are sure you are not feeling any ill-effects?" he demanded, and waved a derogatory hand towards the dinner tray gleaming with silver dishes. "This idea of dining in your room – did you not feel well enough to join the others downstairs?"

Venetia was trying to find her voice as she gazed down into the rest of her coffee, apparently unmoved to outward appearances. Inside her heart was beating like a sledgehammer telling her that thick strange note in his deep voice was because of his concern for herself.

"I'm perfectly well," she said with some semblance of calm. "I felt it was the right thing to do to leave you with some privacy after what's happened. I had no desire to intrude upon what didn't concern me."

"Not concern you? Of course it concerns you. Had it not been for you Isabel would not have recovered so quickly. Indeed, it is quite possible that she might not have recovered at all."

"I can't believe that."

"It is true, nevertheless," he stated with a faint ring of irony in his voice. "Isabel would not have gone to see the carnival had you not been there to go with her. I would not have included her in the house party to be the cynosure of all eyes. You must take the credit for this small miracle."

She felt the hot colour rise in her temples. "But the knock on the head could have occurred at any time. The accident just happened."

He frowned and pushed his hands into his pockets. "That is what puzzles me. Federico is an excellent driver, yet he must have been driving carelessly to lose control and allow the car to go over as it did. He gives no explanation at all."

Venetia relaxed a little at his words. So Federico had made no mention of Isabel's part in the accident. There had been no reason why he should except to clear himself. It was noble of him to shield Luisa, who had kept the knowledge of Isabel's violence and migraine a secret. The maxim of least said soonest mended was an admirable one, Venetia thought, and she admired Federico for his common sense and for being a man. But while Federico had acted completely in character, she was puzzled at the way Ramón was taking Isabel's recovery. To her he looked like a man holding himself in check, exercising great restraint when he should have been on top of the world with joy.

Had Isabel's recovery only brought him more problems to solve? Was he now considering the shock he might give her by confessing he loved Carolyn? She lifted her eyes, but the moment they met his that overwhelming confusion came upon her again sweeping away all her defences.

She collected herself to answer him. "I think you ought to accept what has happened without question and with gratitude. It was meant to be and I am very happy about it. And now your *novia* is quite well again my services here are no longer required." Her fingers curled round her coffee cup in desperation as she forced the words from her lips that would part them for ever. "I would like to leave as soon as it can be arranged."

It was a relief now that she had said it. It had been bothering her all evening how best to end the impossible situation in which she now found herself since Isabel would have no further use of her services. The uncertainty had been checking all her gladness. She sat slim and upright, braced for any argument to change her mind.

Ramón did not speak at once. His regard remained perfectly steady. There was something about him, a ruthlessness, that appalled her gallant struggle for freedom.

When he spoke there was a depth in his voice that was scathing. "So you who have always professed to love a person are now ready to desert that same person in her hour of need." He went on rapidly. "Do you not see that Isabel will need you during the next few weeks more than ever? Where are all those plans of yours gone to invite her friends to the Villa to tea? Isabel will still need your support when she meets them in different circumstances. Those small gatherings will help in building up her confidence when she has to face bitter commitments at the Quinta. Regaining her former intelligence is one thing, helping her to fill in the gap left by her illness is another." He gave a typical Spanish shrug. "Who knows how she will react? There is the possibility that she might not want to leave the seclusion of the Villa. She might even refuse to meet people. You could help her enormously in that direction. You have achieved so much with her already."

Venetia shivered. This was something she had not expected. He was right in what he said, yet could he not do the same for Isabel as he was asking her to do? Once again she had to make a decision with the cold certainty that this time it would affect her whole future. He was speaking again.

"Was it only your compassion for a sick person that persuaded you to stay in the first place?" he demanded satirically. "Do you no longer care what happens to Isabel?"

She lifted her chin militantly. "I care," she answered. "I also understand. I'll stay."

His deep breath was audible and he straightened to smile down on her faintly.

"*Gracias*, Venetia, I am deeply indebted to you. One word more before I go. I want you to promise me that you will contact Doctor Fontera should you feel at all unwell in the next few days. I have known cases of delayed concussion caused by such accidents. You will give me your word that you will do that?"

She was silent for a moment, put off by the dark eyes which seemed to be probing into her very soul.

Then with difficulty she answered him. "I give you my word. You're right about Isabel. Only . . ." She hesitated.

"Yes?" he said.

Again she hesitated, but only for a moment. "You can help her as much as I. Love can work miracles."

He still looked at her keenly, but all emotion had gone from his face.

"I can give her a helping hand, certainly. But you will be the stick she will lean upon. *Buenas noches*, Venetia, sleep well."

Venetia drank the rest of her coffee. It was as cold as her heart. While she was sincere in her desire to do her best for Isabel she knew that her promise to do so would cost her more than one sleepless night.

CHAPTER TEN

VENETIA found life at the Villa irrevocably changed. Isabel's recovery had opened up a new world of emotion. If Isabel was different Venetia had changed too. Or perhaps Venetia in her own unhappiness was turning to the undemanding kindness of Isabel. Perhaps in helping Isabel's rehabilitation she was unconsciously helping her own. She felt, even while she did not fully understand, the delicate fabric of emotion that Isabel was clinging to, so she led her gently into a strange new world, filling each day with a series of pleasures, aided and abetted by beautiful surroundings.

Venetia taught her to swim and they spent every morning before breakfast on the beach happy as sandboys. After the noon siesta they entertained guests for tea. Within the cool interior of the Villa they would chatter to Venetia, Isabel joining in like the rest. Beams of sunlight forced their way across the room between the shutters to reflect on the silver tea service and the blue-black hair and red lips of young women who appeared to have been fed solely on grapes and sunshine.

The house-party at the Quinta had broken up the day following Isabel's miraculous recovery, with Ramón's relatives arriving post-haste at the Villa to see for themselves that his *novia* had indeed recovered. They had gone away of the opinion that the age of miracles had not yet passed, leaving Venetia and Isabel convulsed with laughter at their astonishment.

Doña Matilde and Federico along with Don Jorge and Carolyn had been the last to call. They were on their way home and had called to say goodbye. Carolyn brought with her the Spanish shawl with hardly a word of thanks for the loan of it. It was easy to see that she was terribly disappointed at Don Jorge's decision to return home with Doña Matilde and Federico. She took it for granted that Venetia would now shortly be returning to London, and she had suggested that she applied for the job she had wanted her to take.

"Let me know when you arrive home," she had whispered in an aside as they said goodbye. "I'll ring up George and put in a good word for you."

Mentally, Venetia had shaken her head at her sister's persistence and had said nothing.

As Isabel's confidence returned it was natural that her interest in clothes returned too. With the delight of a child, she pored over the lastest fashion magazines with Venetia and cast out her entire wardrobe to replenish it with a new one. They went to Barcelona to the salons and chose from the fashion shows there the kind of clothes which made her coo with delight when they eventually arrived at the Villa.

Isabel's greatest delight however, appeared to be the receiving and answering of her correspondence. After breakfast each morning she would be busy at the small writing table in the salon at the Villa, leaving Venetia with the freedom to do as she liked until lunch time. She welcomed those brief hours of solitude when she would take a stroll in the grounds and try to make plans for when she was no longer needed at the Villa. But the beauty around her had dimmed since Ramón was no longer at the Quinta.

No one knew where he had gone. It was just possible that he had gone to stay with Don Jorge to be near to Carolyn. If not, then Carolyn, shut up in Don Jorge's villa typing out his memoirs, was probably feeling dispossessed indeed. Venetia longed for yet dreaded his return. Then, as his absence lengthened into weeks, she began to relax. The household at the Villa became a happy one as Isabel continued to become more alive and alert to her surroundings. Angelina had now changed the usual repertoire of songs she ran through in the kitchen, and instead of her mournful dirges light love songs were now to be heard when Venetia passed her kitchen on the way to the garden. Rodrigo appeared to be spending more time tending his prize blooms while keeping a wary eye on the orange blossom. Even Luisa hummed a little these days.

One evening Federico arrived unexpectedly in his car. He had called on his way back home after collecting the rest of Don

Jorge's writing equipment from the Quinta, and he stayed to dinner. It was a happy meal, with Federico at the top of his form. Venetia was pleased to see he had lost the haunted look so apparent between spurts of gaiety which he had hitherto worn. He said that Carolyn and Doña Matilde sent their regard to Venetia and that they were all dining out that evening with friends. No mention was made of Ramón and Venetia wondered why Isabel did not enquire about him.

At ten o'clock Venetia went to her room, aware that, since Federico was family, he might have something private in that respect to say to Isabel. The good food and wine plus the gay company of Federico and Isabel had made her sleepy, and in no time at all, as her head touched the pillow, she was asleep.

When she awoke the following morning sunlight was streaming into the room and there was someone knocking imperatively on her door. When it flew open, Luisa was standing there looking as though she had seen a ghost. Her sallow face looked strangely yellow and she held a letter in her hand.

"It's Señorita Isabel, Miss Mellor," she cried agitatedly. "She's gone!"

"Gone?" Venetia stared at her in bewilderment. "Gone where?" she asked weakly, pushing herself up into a sitting position in bed.

Luisa shook her head. "I do not know. Her bed has not been slept in, and her clothes have gone along with her suitcases."

With sudden shock Venetia heard Luisa's announcement with a confused sense of something willed by the hand of fate. Was it possible that . . .? But no, she would not believe it. Surely they would never go without telling her?

She looked hopefully at Luisa. "Are you sure she's not playing some prank on you and is even now hiding in her room?"

The reply was emphatic. "It is no prank, Miss Mellor, as you can see by this letter. It is for you. There is another one for the Señor Conde. Rodrigo has taken it to the Quinta."

Venetia left her bed and shrugged into a wrap, tying the girdle around her waist with shaking fingers. Then she guided Luisa to a chair.

"Do sit down," she said gently. "May I see the letter?"

The envelope was addressed to Miss Mellor in a fine, precise hand.

"*Ventia, querida hermana,*" Isabel had written. "I am going away with Federico. We are going to be married. I have left a letter for Ramón. I am sorry to have to leave you like this without saying goodbye. I say it now with love and a deep gratitude for all you have done for me. We shall meet again some day, that I know. Until then, as always, your sister, Isabel."

Venetia read the letter again aloud to Luisa before returning it to the envelope. Then with more assurance than she felt, patted the stiff shoulder of Luisa, who sat bolt upright in her chair.

"Isabel will be all right with Federico," she said gently. "They love each other. I'm sure you will be hearing from her soon. Your Señorita Isabel could never do without her Luisa."

Luisa nodded comprehendingly and, rising slowly to her feet, walked with dignity from the room. It was Venetia's turn to sink into a chair when she was alone. So Isabel had gone! Those letters she had written each day at her writing table had been mostly to Federico. They had made their plans by correspondence and had taken their chance while Ramón was away. They had gone, leaving the way clear for Carolyn to marry him. There would be no more companionable get-togethers for her and Isabel, no more scrambles on the beach playing together like children in a seventh heaven of sea, and hot sun. Those solitary walks taken when Isabel was busy at her writing table would be no different from all her other walks from now on.

Venetia stared down at the letter still in her hand. To her it was as good as a passport to home. There was no reason for her to stay on at the Villa any longer. She would pack immediately after breakfast. Pain rose inside her at the thought of leaving Spain never to see Ramón again. He would no doubt invite her over to the Quinta when he and Carolyn were married, might even go to London, but Venetia would take good care that they never met again unless it was in a large gathering where she could move about and assume a gay exterior.

She was still sitting there staring into space when Angelina brought her breakfast. There was a new air of excitement about Angelina, her round, pleasant face was wreathed in smiles. Spanish fell bubbling from her lips as she put down the tray. Was it not romantic, this elopement of the Señorita Isabel? Everyone was sorry for the Señor Conde who was so *hermoso* and *simpatico*. But, a shrug, was not Don Federico also *atractivo* and *simpatico* too? Just imagine being carried away by a lover to be married! The dark eyes sparkled. Venetia listened, tried to keep up with the Spanish and felt exhausted when, at last, Angelina said, "May God bless them," as she made the sign of the cross.

After breakfast Venetia began her packing, flicking open the locks of her two suitcases with tired, dragging movements and folding her clothes mechanically. It would not be wise to ask for the car from the Quinta, since to do so would only be to invite more gossip. Everyone at the Quinta would be sure to have heard by now of Isabel's elopement. She would ask Luisa about the nearest garage.

Luisa was very upset to see her go and wiped her eyes with the corner of her apron. Yes, she knew of a garage where Miss Mellor could hire a car and a driver. But upon enquiring, Venetia was told that it would be a matter of two hours before a car would be available. She put down the receiver and looked at her watch. Two hours could be an interminable time when one was in a hurry to be gone. Slowly she walked to the door leading out on to the patio, then stopped, putting a startled hand to her throat. A tall figure filled the doorway silhouetted darkly against the sunlight.

"Hello, Venetia," said a familiar deep voice. "Did I startle you?"

For several breathtaking moments she was without speech and could only stare wide-eyed at the tall, teak brown figure who, while he looked strong, was far too lean.

"Julian!" she cried with joy and surprise, and flung herself at him. "How lovely to see you! How are you?"

She laughed up into his face, loving the old warm friendliness kindling in his eyes.

"Fine," he answered, taking in the glow of her rising colour beneath the smooth peach tan of her cheeks and the tawny hair sequined with golden glints in the rays of the sun slanting through the doorway. "How are you?"

"I'm fine." She hugged him and then stepped back to take his hands. "Have you seen Carolyn?"

He shook his head. "I only arrived at the Quinta an hour ago. I expected to see her there."

"Carolyn's gone back with Don Jorge to Santa Marta," she told him. "Disappointed?"

He squeezed her hands. "It wouldn't be very gallant of me to say so since you're here. I've come to ask you to have lunch with me at the Quinta.

Slowly Venetia freed her hands from his and said awkwardly, "I'm sorry, Julian, I can't. I'm all packed ... waiting for a conveyance to take me to Barcelona. I'm leaving Spain."

He raised his dark brows in astonishment. "Now, this minute?" he demanded, and consulted his watch on a deep frown. "What time does your plane leave?"

Venetia clasped her hands loosely in front of her and spoke down to them. "I'm hoping to be lucky enough to get a last-minute cancellation."

His frown deepened. "Then if you haven't to catch a plane, why the hurry?"

He bent his head to catch the quiet reply. "My job here is finished. I'm going home."

"So am I when I've seen Carolyn," he answered thoughtfully, "Look, why not travel to Santa Marta with me, then we can go home together? We can have lunch first at the Quinta to sustain us for the journey. What do you say?"

Suddenly Venetia was ashamed for being so self-centred. She had forgotten that Carolyn would probably tell Julian that she was in love with Ramón and that they were going to marry. Julian would be very cut up about it and he would need companionship on his journey home.

175

She smiled up at him. "That will be fine," she agreed. "Did you walk from the Quinta?"

He nodded.

"Then we can use the hired car when it arrives and pick my luggage up from here. All right?" she queried.

Again he nodded.

They were strolling arm in arm towards the Quinta when he said jokingly,

"When you first refused to come to the Quinta for lunch, I thought you were shy at being alone with two men."

Venetia gulped and her fingers tightened on his arm. "Did you say two ... two m-men?" she stammered.

His glance mocked her dismay. "Of course. I came back with Ramón. He wrote to me some time ago asking me to come to the Quinta on a matter of importance, and I came as soon as I had completed my business in Canada. As a matter of fact Ramón and I met at the airport here when our planes landed from different flights. By the way, Simon sends his love with a message." He tossed her a second glance. "Want to hear it?"

"Of course."

"He says to tell you that if you aren't married within the next six months, he's coming over to marry you himself."

"Dear Simon! How is he? Making a go of it, I suppose. Like you, he's the dogged type."

"Yes," he drawled, "as a matter of fact he's doing very well. Wants me to go out and join him."

Venetia swallowed on a dry throat. She could see him doing just that when he heard about Carolyn and Ramón. She wondered whether it was her duty as his friend to soften the blow by a hint, but somehow she shrank from hurting him. Maybe he would take it better from Ramón. In that moment she both loved him and hated him for what he was doing to Julian.

Her attention wandered as Julian told her about Simon and his farm. She was wearing her smart little suit and the matching white accessories she had travelled to Spain in, and was all ready to get away immediately after lunch. Thank goodness Julian would be as eager as she was to get away when Ramón had told them everything.

They entered the great hall of the Quinta much too soon and Venetia drew her hand from Julian's arm to give an unnecessary tug to the jacket of her suit and a nervous pat to the top of her white hat. Julian observed her actions with amusement.

"I'll have to freshen up," he said. "I won't be long. You'll find Ramón in the library."

Unconscious of her utter dismay, he made short work of crossing the hall to take the stairs two at a time.

Venetia stood stock still in the middle of a sea of richly tiled floor, glancing around like a hunted thing at the Persian carpet murals on the walls and wishing some genie would appear and sail her away on one into the unknown.

She was considering whether to sit on the stairs and wait for Julian to appear again when a voice spoke to her left.

"*Buenos dias*, Miss Mellor. The Señor Conde awaits you in the library. This way."

The manservant led her to the double doors to the left of the stairs and flung them open to announce her. Then he was softly closing the door again behind her.

"Come, sit down, Venetia," said Ramón, drawing out a chair near to the heavily carved table on which his opened correspondence was piled neatly. "How are you?"

"Very well, thank you," she replied, taking off her shoulder bag and putting it down on the carpet beside her as she sat down.

He had strolled over to a cabinet to extract a bottle of wine and glasses, while she took off her gloves and laid them on the top of her bag. He raised his eyes from his task for a moment, and a curious thrill shot through her. His look pierced through to her nervousness, but gave nothing away.

He filled the glasses and offered her one, and the next moment her hat was lifted from her hair.

"This, I think, can be dispensed with," he said coolly, putting it down on the carved table. Then, leaning back against it, he lifted his glass.

"I propose a toast to Isabel and Federico. Cheers."

Venetia was beginning to feel very odd. He did not look angry.

He did not look surprised. He did not look anything. She drank and discovered that she was drinking champagne. It seemed to loosen her tongue.

"You know?" she said calmly.

"I have the letter here," he said drily, and as he indicated the pile of opened letters, he put down his glass, reached out for hers and put it down beside it. "Were you surprised to hear about their elopement?"

He had curled his fingers on the top of the table as he leaned back against it and looked at her intently. He was much too near for her comfort and she dropped her eyes away from his smouldering gaze to stare down at the crapet.

"Very much," she admitted. "Poor Luisa was quite overcome. When I recovered from the news I began to realize that I should have expected it because Federico has loved Isabel for a long time. He told me so in secret. I ... I suppose there's no harm in telling you about it now."

His eyes narrowed. "You like Federico?"

She nodded. "Very much. I admire him greatly too, for ... for ..."

He cut in sharply, "For snatching my bride from beneath my nose? Is that what you are trying to say?"

The colour rushed up warmly beneath her clear skin. "I'm sorry, I shouldn't have said that," she rushed on inadequately. "It ... it isn't very nice for you, I know."

He threw back his head and laughed and she stiffened indignantly.

"I know that was an understatement, but you needn't laugh about it. It only goes to show that you don't love Isabel half as much as Federico does. You proved that by going away the moment she recovered, and staying away too," she cried accusingly.

"So I did. And do you know where I went?" He leaned forward, bringing his face very near, and watched her with deep, dark eyes that held so many secrets and told so few, as he continued, "I went in search of Isabel's father who, after losing his wife, shirked his responsibilities to his only daughter and went abroad. It has taken me all this time to find him."

Venetia digested this in silence, then lifted clear eyes to his face.

"Well?" he demanded. "Are you not curious as to why I should seek out such a man?"

She moistened dry lips. "You wanted to tell him about Isabel's recovery, I suppose."

Ramón gestured with a derogatory wave of a hand. "Nothing of the kind," he said curtly. "I would have said you knew me well enough to be aware of the manner of man I am, yet you can see me doing something which is completely out of character." His mouth set and his nostrils flared. "Can you imagine me going half way round the world to seek out a man to tell him news of a daughter he cares so little about that he left her to the mercy of someone else? Do you think that I'm even the kind of weak-kneed idiot who would also go to ask his permission to marry his daughter?"

Venetia stared at him in bewilderment. She had never seen him so ... so emotionally disturbed, as though she was in some way to blame for his journey abroad. What was he so angry about? Why did he not come out into the open and say the real reason for his actions? Well, he had asked for it. Her voice was not quite steady, but she had to to say it in order to end a scene she was finding unbearable.

She said, "I can only think of one other reason why you should go in search of him. You went to ask him to come back to his daughter as you no longer wished to marry her. In your compassion you decided it would be better for Isabel to have someone belonging near her when you told her the truth."

"Precisely." There was a long pause. Then he said softly, "And now you are in a hurry to leave, since your services with Isabel are no longer required. Had I not sent Julian to fetch you to the Quinta to lunch, you would now be on your way to Barcelona, would you not?"

Venetia said honestly, "Not exactly on my way. I'm ready, though."

"So? The question was irrelevant, since I see you are dressed for the quick ... er ... getaway. One more question. Why did you find it so imperative to leave so quickly and without first saying goodbye?"

Her voice was low and husky. "I have to find another job. It was as simple as that."

He looked at her for a long time. Then, as she felt on the point of screaming, he assumed an air of casualness which she regarded as too relaxed to be real and went to the cabinet to bring out fresh glasses and fill them.

"We shall now drink another toast," he murmured with a flash of good humour. "You will please stand up for this. It is most important."

Thoroughly unnerved by now, Venetia obeyed, wondering how long her shaking legs would support her. This was worse than anything she could have imagined. She could think of no other toast than one to his bride and himself. While she was prepared to accept Carolyn as his wife, she had hoped for more time in which to get used to the idea now that it was almost confirmed.

Hardly aware of what she was doing, she raised her glass. The gleam in his eyes made her shiver slightly. It could be mocking, cruel or a bit of both.

"To my future bride," he said with a new quality in his voice. "To the only woman I have ever wanted to marry."

Shrinking inwardly from the pain his words inflicted, Venetia drank. Then with a very gallant act of bravado, she again raised her glass. "To you, Ramón, and to your future happiness always," she said.

He gave a mocking bow. "*Gracias, querida,*" he replied. "To us."

Venetia drained her glass, thinking his last two words rather odd. But then happiness did odd things to people and Ramón, it seemed, was no exception. She was sure he did not realize that he had called her beloved, sure also that he was not himself as he did something more odd to her way of thinking. He took her empty glass and dashed it with his own into fragments against the fireplace.

Then he covered the distance between them and tilted up her astonished face. His eyes fastened on her softly parted lips as he drew her into his arms. His touch filled her with an ecstasy of delight and an almost unbearably hungry yearning. Small flames ran through her body, setting sleeping fires alight as his lips moved over her face. She heard him whisper endearments and caught the words *destino* and *querida* as her heart thumped in tune with his until she could not distinguish one beat from the other.

When his mouth suddenly found her own it was like an explosion of fireworks in the sky sending down thousands of particles of happiness raining on them deliciously. Venetia was in no state to reason as she resigned herself wholly to the dictates of her heart, knowing that it was against every instinct of her pride. Her lips responded to the demanding passion of his. She wanted to cry, "I love you," but close on the delight came the thought that he was not hers to love. He was Carolyn's.

When he lifted his head passion began to die within her leaving only devastating shame. She had been utterly confused and completely mad, incapable of thinking clearly. Now common sense returned and she fought back the tears.

She set her hands against his chest as his smouldering gaze drew her again closer. "Please, Ramón," she begged. "I know you're feeling grateful because you believe I'm partly responsible for Isabel's recovery and your own subsequent happiness, but I ..." She faltered and shook her head hopelessly, smiling at him through her tears in an effort to find the right words. "What I mean is, you're allowing your gratitude to me to reach overwhelming proportions. Just now you mentioned the word *destino*, and I'm sure that is what it was. Just destiny. Isabel was meant to get well, just as you were meant to marry Carolyn."

"Carolyn?" The scorn with which he spoke her name dismissed her image from between them for all time. "What nonsense is this you are saying?" he demanded, making no attempt to release her from his arms.

Venetia was trembling. "I shouldn't have come," she protested, expecting Julian to enter the room at any moment. "I am leaving after lunch with Julian. Please let me go."

Her struggles to free herself only succeeded in tightening his arms around her. There was a terrible silence. Then he said heavily, "So you love Julian?"

She stared at him stupidly. "I've always loved Julian as a brother. I'm travelling home with him, that's all. Like Isabel, he will need someone to comfort him when he hears about Carolyn."

He went very still. Venetia could not have looked at him to save her life just then. But he forced up her chin and she had to meet his gaze. What she saw there made her tremble. He looked terrible.

He said, "I am sick to death of Carolyn." His voice was like the crack of a whip and made her wince. It seemed that she had never known what anger could be like until this moment. He was entirely Spanish, entirely ruthless with his nostrils flaring, his eyes unfathomable depths of thinly restrained anger and his face thin-lipped and cruel. "Why do you think I sent for Julian if not to take her away and marry her? He should have done it years ago instead of leaving her free to add to my problems."

Completely unnerved by this revelation, she whispered, "You don't know what you're saying."

His eyes blazed. Her heart leapt and quivered within her as she gazed at him mesmerized.

"Do I not?" he demanded. "Did I not hear her with my own ears that day in London talking to a certain Lady Rollsmere over lunch? They had everything planned, those two. According to Carolyn, I was a better proposition than working for Tio Jorge." The quality of his voice thickened. He went on rapidly, "That is why I left London so unexpectedly. When I saw you on the plane I thought you had taken her place temporarily in order to ascertain my future movements."

Again she was disconcerted and the quick blood rushed to her cheeks.

"And your thoughts were justified when Carolyn arrived to take my place," she cried in anguish. "Oh dear! How you must have despised me!"

She strained back against his hold, struggling to free herself, but he held her firmly. "How could you think that of me?" she said wildly. "Let me go. Do you hear? Let me go!"

But his arms were like iron bars. She saw the exultation of his strength in the gleaming black of his eyes and the flash of his teeth as he held her at last palpitating and unprotesting against his chest.

He said grimly, "That is better. Now tell me that you love me, that you were running away because you thought I was going to marry Carolyn and you could not face it."

He waited for her to speak and after a long silence, he whispered in her ear, "There are ways of finding out."

Venetia's face shot up at his words and the room was blacked out as he bent his head and pressed his lips demandingly upon her trembling ones. His kisses bruised her soft lips and she was beyond struggling. It was useless to remind herself that he was a man of experience giving vent to anger and a few other emotions coming from some source of which she was unaware. Yet the magic was such that she delighted in the pain and, to her everlasting shame, found herself responding passionately.

The sun moved into the room, chasing away the shadows, and still they were lost in the magic of lips which could not tear apart. At last Ramón let her go and with a deep exultant laugh swept her up into his arms and sat her down upon the huge carved table. Then he stood before her, smiling into a flushed face rosy from his kisses. His eyes caressed her moving up to her tumbled hair shining like a halo in the slanting sunbeams across the room.

"So you do not love me," he teased. "Dare to deny it after that shameless exhibition just now!"

Venetia gasped indignantly. "I like that!" she protested. "You were a partner to it. Besides, kisses don't mean a thing."

His eyebrows lifted and he looked so devilishly sure of himself that her heart lurched with love. "No?" he said, putting his arms around her. "Allow me to qualify that."

Venetia placed her hands against his chest. "Please, Ramón," she begged. "We must be sensible."

He took her hands and kissed them in turn. "I like it better this way," he said, looking deeply into her eyes.

Her fingers curled around his, and her voice shook with a deep thankfulness.

"I still can't believe that you love me as I love you. How can you when you think what you do about me?"

"Shall I tell you what I think of you? I think that you are the most wonderful thing that has ever happened to me. I must have loved you all those years ago when I teased you so unmercifully over your Spanish," he chuckled.

"Yet you went away then and never contacted us. Why?" she persisted.

"Because I learned on my return home that my parents' dearest wish was for me to marry the daughter of their closest friends, Isabel. I had never been in love or I would never have consented. While you had left a deep impression upon me, you were only a child, and I never forgot you." He held her hands against his chest and said sombrely, "The flat I bought overlooking Hyde Park belonged to a friend of my student days. I went over to London to his wedding. I also paid a visit to Tamor Hall to discover that Julian was in Canada with Simon and that you and your sister had moved to London. I had been wanting very much to see you again and I was making enquiries when I had lunch one day with my friend and his future bride. Carolyn was sitting at the next table hidden by a huge pot of palms. The rest you know. I returned to Spain the day after my friend's wedding."

"And there was I on the plane and you didn't recognize me," she said accusingly.

His look was the indulgent one of a lover. "How could I? It took me some time to recognize the butterfly after remembering the chrysalis. When I did I was lost. My heart had gone for ever in your keeping."

Venetia laughed happily. "Was I so shattering? I don't believe it."

"But then you are a woman, *querida*, while I am very much

184

a man," he said on a quick kiss. "Instead of a freckle-faced, ponytailed, shy little girl, I saw a beautiful young woman with an air of serenity and mischief I found instantly appealing. Soft-voiced, gentle and sweet, you twanged on my heart-strings and reminded me of moonlight nights and all the heaven to be found in a woman's arms. I loved you and resented you for what you were doing to my peace of mind, tied as I was in honour bound to look after Isabel." He kissed her again. "You have an air of glamour about you all the more alluring because you are so unconscious of it."

"Flatterer!" Venetia framed his face with her hands, tenderly feeling a ripple of excitement running up her spine as passion again darkened his eyes. "I love you with all my heart," she told him. "I came happily to Spain to work for Don Jorge leaving Carolyn to start a new job in London with a beauty consultant. I never expected her to come to Spain and claim her job back with Don Jorge." She looked at him anxiously. "You believe me?"

His arms tightened around her and she loved the look of utter happiness on his face.

"How could I not?" he murmured with his lips against her cheek. "You looked so shattered when she calmly announced in this very room that she was taking your place with Tio Jorge that I wanted to sweep you up into my arms there and then, carry you away, and make passionate love to you. Instead, I had to think of some plan to keep you in Spain until I could declare my love for you honourable. I must confess that I had sleepless nights after installing you at the Villa with a mentally retarded *novia*. But I was determined not to lose you."

"Now you have me for keeps," she said, winding her arms around his neck. "You will also have Carolyn for a sister-in-law. Can't we do something for her and Julian?" coaxingly. "I'm sure she loves him. The trouble is Carolyn has become used to high living and views life with Julian as a bit of a comedown. She's very ambitious, that's all."

"I have already done something about it. I have invested in Julian's estate, which means he will have the capital to make it pay. He will take a letter of invitation to our wedding which he will give to Carolyn. I have no doubt at all that she will accept him when he tells her about our agreement," he told her quietly, teasingly.

Venetia had to kiss him then. Relief and happiness washed over her, blurring her senses. His arms tightened round her and his answering kisses told her, "You are my life. We belong together always. *Destino*."

So beneath blue Spanish skies Venetia married her Spanish grandee. In a temperature well over the eighties seven hundred guests drawn from Spanish nobility assembled at the lovely old cathedral church of San Jerónimo in Madrid for the occasion. As it was the custom for the bridegroom's father to buy the bride's wedding dress, Ramón had stepped in to provide it. The result was a superb creation, a white lace dress encrusted with diamonds and pearls, made by those famous couturiers, Herra and Oilero of Madrid.

And so began a day of rich uncounted hours which make the one day in a woman's life a paradise. To Venetia it was the first from an endless store as Ramón's wife. Even so, as she entered the hallowed interior of the lovely old church on Don Jorge's arm, she faltered and her breath caught in her throat at the magnificent gathering waiting for her. Terror washed over her in cold waves from which she emerged outwardly calm and a little scared.

"Federico was right," Ramón said when they were in the car driving away from the church. "You are like a Botticelli angel. When you came towards me down the aisle I had to convince myself, as I am about to do now, that you are really flesh and blood."

Then he did something that she was sure was not usually done in public, even by a Conde. He drew her into his arms and it was surprising how many kisses it took to actually convince him.

THE OMNIBUS
A GREAT IDEA FROM HARLEQUIN
NOW AT RETAIL

A GREAT IDEA!

We have chosen some of the works of Harlequin's world-famous authors and reprinted them in the 3 in 1 Omnibus. Three great romances — COMPLETE AND UNABRIDGED — by the same author — in one deluxe paperback volume.

Joyce Dingwell (2)

The Timber Man (#917)
It was bad enough to have to leave Big Timbers, but even worse that Blaze Barlow should think Mim was leaving for the wrong reasons.

Project Sweetheart (#964)
Alice liked being treated as though she were something special—she privately believed she was. Then Bark Walsh, the project boss, suddenly ended her reign!

Greenfingers Farm (#999)
It never occurred to Susan that circumstances were not as they seemed, and that her well-intentioned efforts as companion, were producing the wrong results!

Mary Burchell

Take Me With You (#956)
Lucy fought hard for a home of her own—but it was her return to the old orphanage that provided the means to achieve it.

The Heart Cannot Forget (#1003)
Andrea didn't take Aunt Harriet seriously about inheriting her estate until she met her aunt's dispossessed and furious nephew Giles and his even angrier fiancee.

Choose Which You Will (#1029)
As companion to old Mrs. Mayhew, Harriet expected a quiet country life—but quickly found her own happiness at stake in a dramatic family crisis.

A GREAT VALUE!

Almost 600 pages of pure entertainment for the unbelievable low price of only $1.95 per volume. A truly "Jumbo" read. Please see the last page for convenient Order Coupon.

Amanda Doyle

A Change For Clancy (#1085)
Clancy hadn't liked the new trustee-appointed manager of Bunda Down, Jed Seaforth—but when Johnny Raustmann threatened him she somehow found herself emotionally involved.

Play The Tune Softly (#1116)
Ginny's joy in her new job at Noosa was shattered when she found Jas Lawrence there—the one man she never wanted to see again.

A Mist In Glen Torran (#1308)
There'd been many changes at Glen Torran, but Verona was dismayed to find Ewan MacKinnon still expected to inherit her along with his brother's estates.

Iris Danbury

Rendezvous In Lisbon (#1178)
Janice Bowen went into the impossible Mr. Whitney's office to resign. Instead, she found herself agreeing to accompany him on a business trip to Lisbon!

Doctor At Villa Ronda (#1257)
Nicola usually ignored her sister Lisa's wild suggestions, but this time accepted her invitation. She arrived in Spain to find that Lisa had mysteriously disappeared.

Hotel Belvedere (#1331)
Andrea took on a job at the luxury hotel where her aunt was head housekeeper, only to find her life becoming increasingly and dangerously complicated.

HARLEQUIN OMNIBUS

A Jumbo Read !!!

Elizabeth Hoy

Snare The Wild Heart (#992)
Eileen had resented Derry's intrusion to make a film of the island, but she realized now that times had changed and Inishbawn must change too!

The Faithless One (#1104)
Brian had called her love an interlude of springtime madness but Molly knew that her love for him would never quite be forgotten.

Be More Than Dreams (#1286)
Anne suddenly realized her love for Garth was more important that anything else in the world—but how could she overcome the barrier between them.

Roumelia Lane

House Of The Winds (#1262)
Laurie tricked Ryan Holt into taking her on safari despite his "no women" rule—but found it was only the first round she'd won!

A Summer To Love (#1290)
"A summer to love, a winter to get over it," Mark had once joked. But Stacey knew no winter would help her get over Mark.

Sea Of Zanj (#1338)
A change of scenery, a little sun, a chance for adventure—that's what Lee hoped for. Her new job didn't work out quite that way!

LOOK WHAT YOU MAY BE MISSING

Listed below are the 26 Great Omnibus currently available through **HARLEQUIN READER SERVICE**

Harlequin Reader Service

ORDER FORM

MAIL COUPON TO → Harlequin Reader Service,
M.P.O. Box 707,
Niagara Falls, New York 14302.

Canadian **SEND** Residents **TO:** → Harlequin Reader Service,
Stratford, Ont. N5A 6W4

Harlequin Omnibus

Please check Volumes requested:

☐ Essie Summers 1   ☐ Essie Summers 2   ☐ Amanda Doyle
☐ Jean S. MacLeod   ☐ Catherine Airlie   ☐ Rose Burghley
☐ Eleanor Farnes   ☐ Mary Burchell 1   ☐ Elizabeth Hoy
☐ Susan Barrie   ☐ Sara Seale   ☐ Roumelia Lane
☐ Violet Winspear 1 ☐ Violet Winspear 2 ☐ Margaret Malcolm
☐ Isobel Chace   ☐ Rosalind Brett   ☐ Joyce Dingwell 2
☐ Joyce Dingwell 1 ☐ Kathryn Blair   ☐ Anne Durham
☐ Jane Arbor   ☐ Iris Danbury   ☐ Marjorie Norell
☐ Anne Weale   ☐ Mary Burchell 2

Please send me by return mail the books which I have checked.
I am enclosing $1.95 for each book ordered.

Number of books ordered _____ @ $1.95 each = $ _____

Postage and Handling = .25

TOTAL $ _____

Name _____

Address _____

City _____

State/Prov. _____

Zip/Postal Code _____

VW 130 260